Massacre at Milo Creek

Marshal Tovey had a quiet life at Newton Crossing – at least until the Indian raids began. Somebody was supplying them with guns and the town began to get angry. Soon the situation erupted into violence. Tovey lost control despite a shoot-out with the supplier of the guns and the mob took over with a raiding party headed for the Indian reservation at Milo Creek.

Then there was another raid, but a different one this time, and the town found itself in worse trouble. Could the local preacher and a drunk somehow help Marshal Tovey to restore law and order? Whatever the outcome much lead would fly and blood would be spilt.

Massacre at Milo Creek

WILL PARR

A Black Horse Western

ROBERT HALE · LONDON

© Will Parr 2001
First published in Great Britain 2001

ISBN 0 7090 6806 9

Robert Hale Limited
Clerkenwell House
Clerkenwell Green
London EC1R 0HT

Typeset by
Derek Doyle & Associates, Liverpool.
Printed and bound in Great Britain by
Antony Rowe Limited, Wiltshire

ONE

Wally was always drunk by midnight. His rheumy old eyes were half closed as he sat on his patient mule to let it take him home. A large brown jug of corn whiskey was still tightly clasped in his arms as he crooned gently to the movement of the animal in the bright moonlight.

His hut was on the edge of town. It was a small, sod-covered building with a warped wooden frame that just about kept out the weather. The old man had spent the last twenty years there; ever since his wife had died and his three sons had gone off to fight for the North and never come back again.

He did a little work for his few dollars. The preacher kept him busy cleaning at the meeting-house, and he did some gardening for a few of the house-proud ladies of Newton Crossing. It was enough for a jug of corn mash now and then and a bit of food for himself and his dog.

The moon was high as he reached the outskirts of the little town. He could vaguely see the low range of hills as black silhouettes on the horizon. The little river from which the town got its name was like a silver thread in the foreground. There were figures moving along the top of the hills, and he blinked several times to remove them from his vision. Indians could not exist so close to town. He pulled at the reins to stop the mule while he steadied his body in the saddle.

They were there, sure enough. A line of dark shapes with feathers in their hair and lances proudly pointing to the cloudless sky. Their horses trotted silently along the ridge from right to left, and Wally knew that he was not seeing the sort of things he had occasionally seen in the past. These were real men; armed and dangerously close to town.

He swallowed noisily. There were no Indians nearer than Milo Creek, and that was close to twenty miles away. The law also stopped the other tribes from coming this side of the Powder River. All their reservations were to the west and they had given no trouble for years. He wiped his watering eyes and looked again. The column of a dozen or so dark shapes gradually vanished over the ridge and the moon shone brilliantly on a motionless world.

Wally unstoppered the jug and raised it to his lips. Then he changed his mind and turned the

6

mule round. The animal resisted his use of the rein. It was accustomed to taking him home without guidance and found the sudden change of pattern difficult to understand. It was almost as if the rider was sober, and that never happened after midnight.

They got back to the main street of Newton Crossing a few minutes later and Wally dismounted outside the marshal's office. He tethered the animal and ignored the reproachful look it gave him. There was still a light on as he entered the brick-built jailhouse with a slightly shaky gait.

Marshal Tovey was drinking coffee and just about contemplating going to bed. The town was quiet. All the drunks had gone home, while the only regular troublemaker was laid up nursing a broken leg that the marshal had delivered a couple of days earlier. He groaned aloud when he saw Wally open the door to make his way unsteadily into the office.

'And what can I do for you at this time of night?' Will Tovey asked suspiciously.

He was a youngish, thick-set man with a sunburnt, cheery face and plentiful dark hair that fell low over his forehead. An experienced lawman but short on patience with drunks like Wally Finlay.

'I saw Injuns, Marshal!'

The lawman groaned again and reluctantly put down his coffee-cup.

'All dressed up in feathers and wearin' war paint?' he asked dryly.

Wally blinked. He was not too drunk to know when someone was making fun of him.

'I don't know about the war paint,' he said, 'but I sure as hell seen 'em all along the north ridge. Plain as plain, they was, Marshal.'

Will Tovey looked hard at the old man.

'How many?' he asked in a slightly friendlier voice.

'I reckon there was about a dozen. Maybe less, and they was troopin' along in single file towards the west. Could have been on their way back to Milo Creek Reservation.'

Marshal Tovey got up and went to study the map on the wall. The reservation was twenty miles to the west and the Indians were not allowed to leave it. Nor had they caused any trouble for years since being confined there after the Little Big Horn disaster. He tapped the map with a sturdy finger before offering the old man a cup of coffee. Wally took the mug eagerly and slurped down the hot liquid with considerable noise.

'I ain't drunk, Marshal,' he said defensively. 'Swallowed a few drops, maybe, but I ain't skunk-drunk nohow. There I was on my way home when I sees this string of horses up on the ridge. Plain as day, they was. And I'll tell you, man, they sure scared me.'

The marshal rubbed his jaw uncertainly.

'Could be just a few hunters,' he mused. 'They got no business to be over this way, but I reckon they're harmless enough. I'll report it to the military tomorrow.'

'You do that, Marshal, and don't go trustin' them red coyotes. I can remember the old days before Custer got hisself killed and it all came to a head. Them Sioux came down on Newton Crossing in seventy-two and shot up the town somethin' cruel, they did. Killed a lot of decent folk while they was stealin' horses and burnin' along the main street. Terrible times they was.'

'Yeah, but it's all peaceable now and those days is over. Just go home, Wally, and thanks for lettin' me know. I'll take care of it from here on in.'

'You're welcome, Marshal, but take my advice. Don't trust no Indian.'

The marshal showed his visitor to the door and watched as he mounted the mule and headed back once again for his little shack.

The clouds were now obscuring the moon but the lawman had lost his desire for sleep. There was something about Wally's story that made him think the old man was describing things that he had actually seen. It worried him as he started another patrol of the town.

It was quiet and dark, with both saloons closed and the lights out in most of the buildings. Only the noise of bullfrogs and the swishing of bats disturbed the night air. He stopped at the end of the main street to look out at the ridge of hills where Wally had seen the Indians. The shadows were etched sharply as the moon came out again to reflect in the eyes of some creature that skulked past the livery stable searching for an evening meal.

The marshal looked at the slightly pinkish glow on the horizon without taking much notice at first. It was a little over to his right and was a steady colouration, like a rising sun. It was a moment or two before he realized that he was looking at a fire.

Will Tovey hesitated for a moment before running back to the jailhouse and getting out his saddle. He hurried round to the corral and quickly harnessed a surprised roan mare before arming himself to head out in the direction of the blaze. There was only one small farm in that wide area, owned by the Naylor family who had been trying to make a go of it for the last eight years, striving against weather and low prices.

He did not know them well, for they seldom came into town while he did not often have reason to ride out on the range. So far as he knew, there were three small children and they all scraped a bare living from a few cattle, some hogs, as well as the usual local crops.

It was a three-mile ride through the dark valley, only made possible by the strong moon that kept peeping out from amid the scudding

clouds to light the way with its cold brilliance.
The glow got brighter as he neared the farm, and
when the lawman came round a bend in the trail
and breasted a rise, the burning house could be
clearly seen.

The roof had long since collapsed with only two
of the thick wooden walls and the tall chimney
stonework standing proud against the flames.
Sparks flew into the air as odd timbers crashed
into the centre of the pyre. The marshal
dismounted to see where the family were located.
As he did so, an oil lamp exploded with a muffled
bang to add blueish flames to the scene.

'Anyone about?' Will Tovey yelled. There was
no answer, but he called again, walking over to
the barn and pulling open the sagging door.
There were some wisps of smoke in the almost
empty building as he looked up to see a few parts
of the roof beginning to burn from stray sparks
that had blown across from the house.

The marshal ran to the well and pulled up a
bucket of water. He flung it awkwardly up over
the low pitch of the roof, and after a few efforts,
had the small fires under control.

He flung down the bucket to look around.
There were no horses in the corral but he could
see some hogs moving around, disturbed by what
was happening and annoying the roosting poultry. He tried shouting again and then stood
listening for some response.

It came this time. Vince Naylor appeared from the shelter of the corn crop and advanced with a shotgun in his hands. His wife followed, holding the youngest infant while the other two children clutched her skirts, crying softly as they emerged from hiding.

'What the hell are you doin' there?' the marshal asked in surprise. 'That ain't no way to fight a fire.'

'We ain't fightin' no fire, Marshal,' the young man answered angrily. 'We're just tryin' to stay alive.'

Vince Naylor was a tall man, thin but wiry, and in his late twenties. His face was drawn, and his wife reached out one desperate hand to cling to him.

'It was terrifyin', Marshal,' she said in a shrill voice. 'They'd have killed us all if we hadn't hid out in the corn!'

The lawman looked from one to the other.

'Who'd have killed you?' he asked while already guessing what the answer would be.

'The Indians! They came whoopin' in, burned down the house, and stole our horses!'

TWO

They sat in various uncomfortable chairs around Mayor Harris's spacious office. It was on the second floor of his dry-goods store and the smells of the stock permeated upwards to lend a pleasant aroma to the large, sunny room. The mayor was behind his desk, fat and moustached, with scant hair slicked back and a cigar clenched in his chubby fist.

The marshal sat on his right, a stolid and reliable figure, while the town treasurer, who was also the sole banker, sat on the mayor's left. He was a strange figure for a money-lender; stout, like the mayor, but with an open, happy face and a wide smile. His eyes were usually puckered in the folds of flesh, and his bushy grey side-whiskers fluffed out like those of the Austrian Emperor's, whose features appeared so often in the journals. Some unkind folk said that he did in fact model his looks on Franz Josef, but if it were

13

true, he certainly did not model his great belly on His Imperial Majesty.

They all sat looking at Vince Naylor as he told his story in hesitant sentences.

It had taken until dawn to get him and his family brought back to town. The fire had been left to burn itself out since no amount of water could be drawn off quickly enough to cope with it. The marshal had already heard the full story before riding back to Newton Crossing for a four-wheeled rig and some local help to get them away from the stricken farm.

Their cattle were safely out on the range, while the hogs and poultry could forage for themselves. Nothing of their household goods remained and the only personal possessions they now owned were the clothes in which they stood and the old shotgun that Vince Naylor cuddled like a precious relic. They had been moved into Mrs Seddon's boarding-house at the town's expense until something could be sorted out.

Marshal Tovey had contacted the mayor as early as possible and he had also sent a telegraph message to Fort Preece some forty miles away to alert the commander there of the problem. Now the council was assembled to hear the story.

Mayor Harris nodded at the marshal to begin, and the lawman stood up rather self-consciously to address the half a dozen or so town worthies.

'I got a report about midnight that Indians had

been up on the north ridge,' he said. 'Wally Finlay saw them on his way home.'

One of the councilmen laughed loudly. 'Wally's a drunk,' he snorted.

'I agree, but I couldn't afford to ignore him,' the marshal answered impatiently. 'I started to make a patrol of the town, saw a glow in the sky, and rode out fast to Vince's place. Found his house burned down and all his horses run off.'

He glanced at the young farmer as he took his seat again. The marshal preferred to have someone else being the centre of attention.

Vince Naylor shuffled in his chair. 'We was in bed,' he said in a quiet voice, 'and all of a sudden there was this whoopin' and hollerin'. It was real scary. Then there was shootin' all round the yard. The kids started screamin', and so did the wife. I looked outa the window and here was all these Indians, gallopin' around the place, lettin' off their guns and throwin' lighted torches on to the roof.'

'How did you get away?' somebody asked hoarsely.

'Well, they opened up the corral to let out our horses. Then they started chasin' them all over the yard to get 'em rounded up. So I got the family out the back window and into the cornfield. We hid there until the marshal turned up. It was a real frightenin' time we had. We ain't fightin' folk, Mr Mayor.'

The First Citizen nodded sympathetically. He looked at the other members of the council in case anybody wanted to express an opinion. Preacher Ely Thomas shook his head in sorrow and murmured a few words of well-meant consolation. Nobody took much notice and it was the banker, Frank Lesser, who struck a note of practical common sense.

'Well,' he said firmly, 'the marshal has done all that can be done about warning the military authorities, so we have to sit patiently until they choose to arrive. In the meantime, I suggest we recruit several deputies, alert all the outlying spreads, and be prepared for other attacks. I would guess that this is just some drunken spree, but we have to be careeful. I really can't see the peace being broken after all these years.'

'I agree,' the mayor said eagerly. 'The Milo Creek reservation has never given us any cause for concern and old Chief White Cloud, or whatever his name is, is too old to go makin' trouble. It might be as well if we had a word with the agent. What say, Marshal?'

'I aim to do just that, Mr Mayor,' Will Tovey said firmly, 'but the Indian agent is located at Willard and that's nigh on thirty miles. And there's no telegraph there, so it's a long ride. I reckon it might be a good idea to look in on old Jesse Parker before anythin' else. What he don't know about the Sioux and the reservation at Milo

Creek ain't worth knowin'.'

The mayor agreed. 'Good idea,' he said. 'And if he can't help, then you can go on from his place to the Indian agent.'

'A new Indian agent has recently been appointed,' the Reverend Thomas interrupted. 'He is living at the reservation and I believe that his predeceessor was discharged for – er – what one might call accounting discrepancies.'

'You mean that he was a thief?' The mayor snorted. 'Not the first one, either. Well, I reckon that an Indian agent should be where he's needed. All agreed then? Will Tovey rides out to have a word with old Jesse.'

There was a general murmur of agreement but one of the council gave a loud cough that brought everyone to a sudden silence. They all looked at the sour-faced grain-merchant in his dark coat and white stock.

'Jesse Parker is livin' in sin,' he said in a deep voice. 'And with an Indian woman at that. He is not a man for Christian folks to know.'

The preacher smiled benevolently. 'They are married according to Sioux custom,' he said kindly, 'and have been together for nigh on thirty years.'

'It's not a Christian marriage,' the councilman thundered. 'It's an evil union. And a heathen one at that.'

Ely Thomas was not going to be browbeaten by

17

a layman's bigotry. He stood up gallantly to defend the old rancher.

'They are a couple who may be held up as an example of probity and decency,' he said bluntly. 'He has been a good husband and she has been a good wife. Their son is a credit to them and to this territory. If some people choose to look down their noses at them, it speaks more of the mockers than the mocked. I agree with the marshal. Jesse will know if there's any unrest up at Milo Creek. That's where her kin are.'

'That's agreed then,' the mayor said hastily. 'We'll recruit extra patrols for the town, the marshal will pay a visit on old Jesse, and we'll send messages to all the spreads within our area.'

He glanced at the unhappy-looking Vince Naylor. 'You and your family had better stay in town for now,' he went on. 'I reckon we can look after you until things are safe enough to go back home again. When conditions are right, we organize rebuilding your house, and seein' you settled in. Don't worry about it, son. We look after our own.'

There was a murmur of approval, particularly from the older men who could remember the days when Indian raids were a fairly common event.

Marshal Tovey set out the next afternoon. A great deal had had to be done before he undertook a journey that would keep him away from town for several days. He appointed six deputies, allocated

their duties, and waited impatiently for a
message to come in from the fort. It was not very
helpful when it did arrive. There had been no
other reports of Indian trouble and recent visits
to the Milo Creek reservation had found everything normal. A patrol was promised, but the
wording of the message was vague.

He loaded the mule, hitched it behind his
mare, and set out for the small spread that Jesse
ran with the help of his wife. Their son was away,
working cattle in Wyoming where he had settled
down and married. The weather was warm, but
with cloud gathering in the west. The marshal
made good time over the dry and dusty trail,
which needed the spell of rain that seemed due.

He was a worried man. He had looked round
the Naylor farm on the morning after the fire.
Something was wrong with the situation, and he
was not quite sure what it was. He rode thoughtfully, wondering how to approach old Jesse
Parker on the matter. The man could be a little
difficult to deal with, made sensitive by the fact
that his wife was a Sioux, and looked down upon
by the God-fearing settlers of the area.

The marshal spent the night by a small
stream, sleeping soundly and waking automatically with the dawn. He made his ablutions and
put on the coffee-pot while he began saddling the
mare and tying his gear to the mule.

It was the mule that alerted him. Its large ears

suddenly pricked up as it looked over his stooping shoulder. He turned quickly to spot a slight movement some forty feet away. There were bushes that quivered slightly in the still air and the animal had sensed or seen something that drew its attention.

The marshal drew his gun and moved round to the other side of the mule. He now had some cover from an ambush and he walked the beast of burden further away from the group of bushes. While he did so, he carried on pretending to work at packing his sleeping gear. The bushes moved again and Will Tovey decided to take action.

He levelled the pistol over the mule's back and fired two shots at extreme range. He did not really expect to hit anything, but it would at least produce results.

The animal bucked at the sudden explosions and the clump of bushes shook violently. Three figures sprang from cover and darted down the slope after one of them fired a wild shot. They ran towards a large outcrop of rock as the marshal cocked his gun again and hurried after them to get within range. He fired once more and splinters flew off the outcrop. They vanished from sight, and before he could move another five yards, he heard their horses galloping away.

He ran round the edge of the outcrop and could see them making off in a westerly direction, their brown bodies glistening in the early sunlight. He had been stalked by three Sioux braves armed with Winchesters.

THREE

Jesse Parker's small cattle-ranch was in a deep valley, made fertile by a narrow stream that came icily down from the nearby hills. He had a low, sprawling house with a stone chimney at each end. It was built of logs with a roof turfed over to grow a foot-high crop of lush grass that a family of goats could reach with the aid of a water-butt, and considered to be their private pasture.

Jesse came to the door to greet the marshal. He was a broad man, bent now with age and work, and his face as dark as that of an Indian. It was lined and unshaven and he wore a thick flannel shirt with baggy pants that were neatly patched.

'Nice to see you again, Will,' he said warmly. 'There ain't many visitors in these parts. Come in and have some dinner. I've got the best food for a hundred miles in any direction.'

After the marshal's animals had been dealt with, the two men entered the house where

22

Jesse's wife was laying out the plates on the scrubbed, white table. She smiled at the marshal and went back to the stove where the pleasant aroma of cooking filled the room as she removed the lid from a large iron pan.

'That sure smells good,' Will Tovey said appreciatively.

'My Mary was always a good cook,' Jesse cackled. 'I keeps tellin' her it's the only reason I took her to wife.'

He pushed the marshal into a chair and sat down opposite while his wife began dishing up the meal. She moved silently, a stout woman in a plain gingham dress that looked store-bought. Her greying hair was pulled back in a tight bun and her placid, unlined face made her look younger than the near sixty years she had to be.

'I'll be takin' it that this ain't just an afternoon stroll you'll be takin', Will,' old Jesse said as they ate.

The marshal told him about the raid on the Naylor place and of the three Sioux who had trailed him. Jesse looked at the impassive face of his wife before answering.

'And you wondered what I know of the doings at Milo Creek reservation?' he asked.

'I thought you might be able to help, yes.'

'Well, Mary and I was up that way about six, seven weeks ago. One of her kin had just died and we went along to pay our respects.' The old man

23

held out his tin mug and waited while his wife
silently filled it with fragrant coffee. 'If there'd
been any sort of unrest there, I'd sure have seen
it. They're peaceable people, Will. Old White
Cloud is like me. He wants a quiet life, and as long
as his folk are fed, he don't go raisin' no trouble.'

He took the after-dinner pipe from his wife's
hand and lit it with the paper spill she gave him.

'I ain't sayin' as how they don't take the odd
steer that roves too far, and I ain't sayin' as how
some of the young fellas don't go gettin' drunk on
corn mash now and then. But there's no more to
it than that.'

The marshal nodded agreement. 'That's always
been my view,' he said, 'and that's why I'm
worried, Jesse. Are there any other groups of
Indians in the area?'

'No, they was all cleared out or forced on to the
other reservations across the Powder River. You
certain sure it was Indians?'

The marshal hesitated for a moment before
pulling out a collection of .44 cartridge cases from
his waistcoat pocket.

'I got my suspicions,' he said as he laid them on
the table. 'Some of the horses that were around
the Naylor place were unshod. That would make
it an Indian raid. On the other hand, these cases
were ejected from carbines. Have the Milo Creek
Indians gotten themselves any Winchesters?'

Old Jesse shook his head. 'Nary a one. You

know better than that, Will. They got Spencers
and a few old Springfields, but no modern guns,
and nothin' that'll fire that sort of ammunition.
The army have seen to that.'

'What about some crooked Indian agent
supplyin' them?'

Jesse grinned and shook his head. 'There ain't
none around no more. Colonel Gross knocked it
all on the head. He suggested to Washington that
they place a preacher at Milo Creek. Them poor
Indians have got the Reverend Blackett borin'
the souls out of 'em now. And he don't hold with
guns in the hands of his flock. All they got, Will,
is enough fire-power to do a bit of huntin'. You
can lay to that.'

'He must be the fella that Ely Thomas
mentioned.'

'Sure as hell is, and he's out at Milo Creek now.
Settled down right well there, he has. Bert Strode
is back in Washington, waitin' on an enquiry
about his misuse of funds.'

Will Tovey took another sip of coffee and
picked up the little pile of cartridge-cases again.
'Are any of the men missing from the reservation?' he asked.

Jesse Parker did not answer right away. He
glanced at his wife who was sitting by the fire
doing some sewing. Her face was quite impassive
as she caught his look, and her fingers continued
to work rhythmically.

The marshal repeated the question.

'Well, I gotta be fair,' Jesse said slowly. 'Lives might depend on it. White Cloud's son and a couple of other braves are out on the range some place. Been gone two or three months. But it don't signify nothin'. They could be huntin' or visitin' kin in the other reservations back west of here.'

'For two or three months?'

The old man shrugged. 'Young fellas is impetuous, Will. You knows how it is. Besides, some of them have a taste for hard liquor and they swap hides for corn mash.'

'And have they got modern guns?'

'Hell, no. That I'm sure about,' the old man said positively. 'Look, fella, the Sioux have been peaceable for years, and I don't reckon to 'em doin' somethin' bad just for the hell of it. Even if they had burned down the Naylor place, why go after you? It don't make a lotta sense.'

'That's what I'm thinkin', and that's why I'm treadin' careful, Jesse. Gettin' Indians moved off their land for the sake of settlers or ranchers who wanted to grab water or pasture, was a popular trick at one time. That's why I'm thinkin' along those lines. I'd feel happier if these three missin' fellas would turn up though.'

'I figure they will in good time. I'll tell you what I'll do, Will. I'll pay another visit to Milo Creek and feel out the situation. Mary and me can talk to the chief. He's a straight fella. If I get any news for you, good or bad, I'll come into town.'

They agreed on that and the marshal went back on his way soon after. He did not go straight back to Newton Crossing. There were two cattle-spreads that he was going to visit first. They needed to be warned of what had happened so that they would not be taken by surprise.

Fred Mason's ranch was a vast area of well-watered pasture that stretched to the foothills of the eastern mountains, which still bore traces of snow glittering in the sunshine. He was sure of some good food and a night's lodging. Fred Mason was a tall, gangling man whose large family of sons and daughters did most of the work. He and his father had made a fortune during the late war, and the comfort of his home showed their wealth in the store-bought furniture that adorned it.

He listened to the marshal's story with a deep frown on his tanned face.

'I don't reckon the Sioux are like to cause trouble,' he said thoughtfully. 'I've lost an occasional steer, but since they was set up on the reservation, there's never been a problem that gave us a moment's worry. There's more to this than a few drunk Indians, Will.'

The marshal agreed. 'I'm inclined to think so,' he admitted, 'but I can't imagine what it could be.'

'Well, land ain't really worth havin' no more. Nobody wants to expand at the moment,' Fred Mason said. 'The price of beef is down and there's no sign of things gettin' better. There ain't no gold or silver to be had around here either. It might be just a few braves puttin' on a show.'

'I hope so, and old Jesse Parker tells me that three of 'em are missin' from Milo Creek. Let's just hope you're right.'

Marshal Tovey went on his way the next morning, calling at Matt Stober's smaller spread before heading for home. The weather stayed fine but there was cloud to the east and he hurried to get to Newton Crossing before the storm broke.

It was while he was crossing a small stream that he noticed a flock of birds circling in the far distance. He watched for a moment before realizing that they were vultures, diving and soaring over something that was a potential meal.

Will Tovey turned his mare towards the scene, a distance of about half a mile. The grass was deep, studded with small bushes, and the going flat in the valley bottom. He stopped about fifty yards from the spot where the vultures were landing, squabbling loudly, and then taking off again. He could see the rising backs of a couple of jackals fighting off the birds and tearing at something on the ground.

The marshal advanced with his gun drawn. He stopped to fire a shot in the air and all the crea-

tures scattered as he approached the object
their scavenging.

It was a human being, and the marshal bit his
lip at the sight. The body was not badly torn and
had obviously only died within the last few hours.
It lay on one side, exposing an injury to the back
of the left leg. The wound had been bound with
coarse cloth and a tourniquet had been applied
above the damage. A great deal of blood had
flowed, and it was easy to guess that an artery
had been ruptured. He knelt down and untied the
rough bandage. It showed a bullet wound that
had no exit hole. The lawman took out his knife
and dug for the bullet. It was easy to locate and
he found himself looking at a .44-calibre piece of
lead that had almost certainly come from his own
pistol.

One of the wild shots he had fired at the three
men who had been stalking him, had found a
home.

He wiped the blade of the knife and put it back
in its sheath. There was no doubt about it; the
dead man was a Sioux; a young fellow with an
empty whiskey jar at his side and a Winchester
carbine only a few feet away from his body.

FOUR

'So they were Sioux braves out for trouble,' the mayor said with a frown. 'I was rather hopin' it was something less worryin'. A few white men tryin' to blame the Indians and get them moved off their land, perhaps.'

The marshal was sitting in the mayoral office, sipping good whiskey and enjoying the comfort of one of the better chairs that littered the room.

'Yes, I feel the same way,' he said. 'White men we can deal with, but an Indian war is too serious to think about. It could involve the other reservations. Old Jesse said that three young fellas are missin' from Milo Creek. They could be the ones who tried to bushwhack me. I fired wild and at long range. I must have caught him in the leg by sheer chance and he bled to death. The others couldn't do anythin' for him so he was left.'

'The trouble is, Will,' the mayor said slowly, 'that Wally Finlay said he saw more than three,

30

and there were certainly more than three at the Naylor place. So where do the others come from? And where are they now?'

'And how in hell did they get new Winchesters?' Will Tovey mused. 'Somebody's been supplyin' modern guns, and I don't like that.'

The mayor drummed his fat little fingers on the desk top.

'There is Sid Welland,' he said quietly.

Will Tovey nodded agreement. 'He's certainly got some carbines in stock, but he'd want cash money for them. The Sioux are mighty short on that.' He stroked the side of his face. 'Unless he had some long-term idea like givin' them credit and acceptin' stolen horses as payment.'

Sid Welland had once been an Indian agent in the west of the territory until he was dismissed for supplying whiskey to the people on the reservations. He had taken horses and buffalo hides in exchange and then bought himself a store in Newton Crossing where he sold guns and ammunition. His brother ran a horse-trading business at Miles City where the railroad had just arrived with a great flourish of civic rejoicings.

'I doubt we'll prove anythin' against him,' the mayor said in a tired voice, 'but he'd be happy to start an Indian war if it put a few dollars in his poke. He has a market for stolen horses and cattle through that brother of his, and Miles City is too far away for you to pay a visit.'

'Yeah. I suppose I could telegraph the local law to check the brands if Naylor's animals ever do show up there.'

'I doubt it would help. So, what do we do now, Will?'

'I'll pay his store a visit,' the lawman said as he rose to leave. 'I might just spot somethin' not quite right.'

'Look out for Rico then. He's one mean man.'

The marshal nodded. Rico Edwards was Sid Welland's hired man; a large, ugly gunslinger who was frequently drunk and always looking for trouble.

'I'd love him to cross me,' he said. 'This town would be a lot better without him, and I just need an excuse.'

'Amen to that, but make sure it's all legal.'

The marshal was occupied for the rest of the morning with the minor nuisances that had built up while he had been away. When he had cleared up these few matters and expelled a couple of drunks whom his deputies had lodged in the cells, he strode down the main street to the gunstore owned by Sid Welland.

It was a pleasant place with white board frontage, clean windows, and a large gilded sign that told the world of the biggest stock of Colt, Winchester, and foreign weapons available in the county.

There were no customers and Sid Welland was at the glass-topped counter, unpacking cardboard boxes of ammunition. He was a small man, neatly dressed, and with a thin, bony face that was not helped by a ragged moustache and pale, shifty eyes. The eyes were never still; always on the alert like some hunted animal. The appearance of the marshal was enough to make him start a little as one of the boxes fell from his hand, spilling .44 cartridges noisily around.

The lawman helped him retrieve them and replace the bullets in their container.

'You seem a mite nervous, Sid,' he grinned. 'Got a bad conscience?'

'You will have your little joke, Marshal,' the man answered a shade uneasily.

'I will, won't I? Sold any Winchesters lately?'

'Winchesters?' He sounded as though he had never heard the word before.

'They're carbines,' the marshal explained with a certain malice. 'Used for killin' folk.'

The man grinned in a rather sick way. 'Not a lot of demand at the moment,' he said. 'Why do you ask?'

'I could be in the market for one.'

'Oh.' There was a certain relief as the dealer put away the cardboard boxes on the shelf behind him. 'I have a few,' he said in a more confident voice. 'New or used?'

'Oh, I think the town can afford to buy me a new one.'

Sid Welland moved a few paces along to open a glass wall-case from which he removed a Winchester rifle. He handed it to the marshal with a look of pride.

'Latest model,' he said, 'and you can have it in .38- or .44-calibre. Beautiful gun.'

Will Tovey examined it carefully. He was looking for the maker's number. When he found it, a trace of disappointment darkened his face.

'Nice weapon,' he admitted. He laid it down on the glass counter and leaned across to take a closer look at the boxes of ammunition.

'Let's have a look at those .44 cartridges,' he said softly.

Sid Welland gave him a puzzled glance as he took down one of the blue-labelled boxes. The marshal opened it to remove a bullet while the storekeeper watched him alertly.

'Somethin' the matter, Marshal?' the man asked. 'They're best quality. Made by Remington.'

'Yes, I see that. Only thing is, most of the folk round here use Winchester ammunition.'

'I've got that as well. Just as good.'

Marshal Tovey put the cartridge delicately back into the packet.

'I found a few Remington cases the other day,' he said slowly. 'Fired off by the Sioux who raided the Naylor ranch. Know anythin' about that?'

34

Sid Welland's ferrety little face puckered in fright. He shook his head vigorously.

'I'm an honest man, Marshal!' he protested. 'I never sell Indians guns or ammunition. You should know better than that. My reputation . . . !'

'Your reputation smells like a dead skunk, fella,' the marshal said unkindly. 'You've done plenty of deals with Indians. I recall you sellin' them whiskey and guns ten, fifteen years ago.'

'Single-shot weapons, Marshal. Nothin' more. I'd never supply them with modern guns. Only percussion firearms. Them's the rules, as you very well know.'

'I came across a dead Sioux with one of your new Winchesters,' Will Tovey said as he handed back the cartridge packet. 'Filled with Remington bullets, it was.'

'Well, it's nothin' to do with me. I didn't supply it.'

'Mind if I have a look round?'

The man licked his dry lips. 'What for?' he asked.

'Oh, I was just wonderin' if I might find a few more rifles with maker's numbers somewhere near the ones on the dead Sioux's gun. His was a new piece. Looked like it had never been used much. Maybe I'll keep it for myself instead of buyin' one. After all, his folk are hardly likely to claim it, are they?'

35

Sid Welland was sweating. The beads of perspiration were running down his cheeks and there was a slight twitch at the corner of his mouth. The marshal had no doubt that he was on the right track.

'I'll go and see the mayor . . .' the man began. 'I'm a prominent man in this town and he'll—'

'The mayor sent me,' the marshal pointed out cruelly. 'He don't like Indians from the reservation bein' armed with new guns any more than I do. If he found out who was supplyin' them, it'd be a long time in the county jail for the fella involved. Now, I was askin' about makin' a search.'

'I can't permit it. This is my home. I have rights!'

Before the marshal could say anything else, a door at the back of the store opened and a large man came awkwardly into view. He was dark and unshaven, with a mass of hair that grew low on his forehead. He lurched slightly as he steadied himself against a glass case of hunting-knives. Will Tovey watched him carefully. It was Sid Welland's pet rattlesnake by the name of Rico Edwards.

'You havin' trouble, boss?' the man asked in a thick, slurred voice.

The storekeeper came round the counter and stood between the two men.

'Nothin' I can't manage, Rico,' he said in a pacifying tone. 'The marshal and me is just havin' a little discussion. Unpack them shotguns, will you, and wipe the oil off'n them.'

The man hesitated for a moment, and then turned on his heel to go back the way he had come. He slammed the door behind him as a sign of his contempt for the law.

'He'll get you into trouble, one of these days,' the marshal said. 'Folk like Rico give a place a bad name.'

The store-owner managed a weak smile. 'He's all right. Just needs a bit of managin', Marshal. After all, a little protection is needed in my business. Guns is dangerous.'

'They are indeed. Especially in the hands of Indians.'

Sid Welland spread his hands. 'Marshal,' he said urgently, 'I give you my word that I have never sold Winchesters or ammunition to any Sioux. I'd be endangerin' the whole community. If you want to search, please do. I can't speak more honest than that.'

Will Tovey hesitated. The man seemed almost genuine, and he knew that if he was permitted to search, it was unlikely that any incriminating evidence would be found. He nodded his thanks, took a cursory look around the store, and then went back to the street.

He was crossing towards his office when the preacher caught up with him. The Reverend Ely

Thomas's cherubic face was red with hurrying as he laid an urgent hand on the marshal's arm.

'I'd like a little of your time, Will,' he said breathlessly. 'In your office perhaps.'

They entered the cool building and the marshal poured out coffee from the pot that had been simmering away on the stove. It was as strong as an angry bull but the stout little preacher drank it manfully. He wiped his mouth and put the mug back on the desk.

'I couldn't help but notice that you were giving Sid Welland a load of hassle,' he said. 'Anything you could tell me about?'

'It was about that raid on Naylor's place. How are they doin', by the way?'

'We've arranged rooms for them in town until we can get some help to rebuild their home and furnish it. What's it got to do with Welland?'

'I was stalked by three Indians when I was visitin' with old Jesse Parker. At least one of them had a new Winchester with the same sort of ammunition that was used around the Naylor's farm. You know Welland's reputation.'

'I surely do, but he hasn't left town in weeks. Nor has Rico. That's what I wanted to tell you when I saw you coming from his store.'

The marshal raised an eyebrow. 'It sounds as if you can tell me a bit more,' he said slowly. 'Are you sure of that?'

The preacher leaned forward in his chair. 'Will, I've had folk watching that store for months. I didn't like to mention it back at the council meeting, but the new Indian agent is a colleague of mine. The Reverend Nat Blackett. He's trying to make sure that no liquor or guns are sold to the Sioux on the Milo Creek reservation. The preachers and church-goers around the area of the reservation are checking the sort of men who might break the law in this respect. We're watching Welland all the time. He and Rico haven't moved out of Newton Crossing for months, and they've only sold guns to local folk.'

'Is that a fact now?' the marshal sighed. 'The funny thing is that I felt he was tellin' me the truth when I spoke to him. Yet he was as scared as hell. If you'll pardon the expression.'

'He's a man with a bad conscience, so any visit from the law is like to upset him. But the fact remains that neither him nor Rico have left town for a long time. And if there was any sign of trouble among the Sioux, Nat Blackett would have been in touch with me and every other churchman around. It all seems very odd.'

'Yes, and I'm wondering. . . .'

The office door opened with a crash and the telegraph operator entered hastily. He pulled up a little when he realized that there was a visitor, but then decided to speak anyway.

'Sorry to butt in, Marshal,' he said in a worried voice, 'but the telegraph has gone dead. Right in the middle of a message for Dugan's store from Fort Preece. I can't get anything in or out.'

Marshal Tovey looked at the little, wispy man with his watery eyes behind nose-pinching glasses. His mop of reddish hair was disturbed by the wind and he ran a thin hand across it in an anxious gesture.

'You think the wires are down?' he asked quietly.

'They sure as hell must be,' the man replied firmly. 'The next terminal is fifteen miles away at Platte Bridge. They're out as well. We'll have to send someone to check the wires in each direction.'

He paused for a moment as he looked hard at the preacher and the lawman.

'Unless it's Indians again,' he said in a dull voice. 'If that's the case, it don't pay to send nobody, I reckon.'

The marshal stood up. He was not sure of his next move but did not intend to look indecisive in front of people who were relying on him.

'I'll start organizin' things right away,' he said calmly.

Before he could do anything else, another figure came through the open door. It was Alf Saunders, a saddler who had a place at the edge of Newton Crossing. The man was pale and carried a shotgun.

'Marshal,' he said urgently, 'there's Indians on the outskirts of town!'

FIVE

Newton Crossing was in a panic. All the side-
streets were barricaded with wagons, piles of
wood, or bales of straw. The main street was
blocked at either end with a string of barrels
backed by overturned gigs behind which the
townsmen were gathering with their guns at the
ready.

Marshal Tovey had allocated positions to each
defendant. He and the mayor hurried around,
making sure that any windows overlooking the
back parts of the town were protected and that
all the outlying corrals were emptied of animals.

There was grim tension in the air as they
waited. Somewhere to the south was a plume of
smoke, and an arrow was found sticking out of
the wooden wall of Molan's livery stable. The
women stood around, ready to load guns and take
care of the wounded or the children. Most of the
youngsters were unconcerned about the danger

and only too happy to have been liberated from the tyranny of education.

The marshal mounted his horse so that he could move from place to place with greater speed. He was sweating, not with the heat, but with the uncertainty of everything.

Somebody let out a yell and all eyes were turned to the southern end of the main street. A group of Sioux were crossing over a ridge in the far distance and stood out blackly in the afternoon sun. Their horses moved swiftly as the sound of their guns floated into town on the light breeze. Will Tovey tried counting their number but the riders galloped wildly, driving loose horses ahead of them as they went. He reckoned on there being at least six, but the gathering dust and constant movement made it very difficult to be sure.

Another shout from the northern end of the street had him galloping in that direction. One of the townsmen pointed out a cloud of dust as the figures of several more red men galloped up a distant slope, firing into the air as they went.

'We got one hell of a situation here, Mr Mayor,' he shouted as he drew up his horse at the jailhouse. 'The telegraph line's down, the red men are out of the reservation, and we got no help comin' from no place!'

'Can we hold them off, Will?' the mayor asked tremulously.

The marshal dismounted. 'Well, I reckon as how there must be near a hundred fightin' Indians at Milo Creek. We can muster almost double that number of men in town. Trouble is that they might be joined by the western braves. And that would be one hell of a lot of firepower.'

'But wouldn't the army have told us if the other reservations had broken loose?'

'I reckon they gave us a gentle hint when I sent that message the other day. They didn't promise no help after the Naylor place was burnt out. Now I figure as how I know why. They already had trouble on their hands and we just don't rate urgent help. They got bigger things to worry about.'

The mayor swallowed noisily. 'Then it's all up to us,' he said quietly. 'We have to manage best we can.'

'I reckon so, Bob. Tell the folk that the army are on the way. Give 'em somethin' to hope for. They'll fight better. And tell Myron Davis to keep his mouth shut about the telegraph line. It's no use causin' folk to fret more than they have to. Outside Myron, only you, me, and the preacher know that we're cut off.'

The mayor nodded and went off to talk to some of the people who were anxious to have his views on the situation. The marshal walked across the street to Sid Welland's gun-store. He led his horse over and tied it to the hitching rail. The owner

was standing in the doorway, his large assistant
at his side. Both men carried Winchesters and
waited stolidly for the lawman to mount the
wooden sidewalk.

'I'll need your help, Welland,' Will Tovey said in
a flat voice. 'Ammunition and guns. And any
dynamite you got.'

'You've changed your tune,' the store-owner
said with a slight hint of triumph. 'One minute,
I'm the villain of your play, the next, you're
screamin' for help. You payin'?'

'Fix all that up with the mayor. But remember
this. If them Indians get into town, they'll take
your scalp just as soon as anyone else's. They
ain't fussy when the killin' mood gets 'em.'

The storekeeper paled a little and looked at
Rico Edwards. The big man stood impassively, his
little eyes staring towards the end of the street.

'You'll have all the help I can give you,
Marshal,' Sid Welland said after a moment's
pause. 'Rico and me will deal out bullets as
they're needed.'

A volley of shots rang out as he spoke. It was a
distant sound that held a note of mockery. The
marshal crossed the street again, leaving his
horse outside Welland's store. He accosted the
little telegraph operator who was standing
among a noisy crowd of irate men whose voices
were rising above all the other sounds on the
street.

'Myron,' the marshal said quietly, 'have you told anybody else about the wires bein' down?'

The man shook his head indignantly. 'I don't talk about telegraph matters, Marshal. You know that. Only you and the reverend knows about it.'

'Good. I aim to keep it that way or we'll have a panic. Now, when these red devils clear off, can you ride out with me and do a repair job?'

The man stared in horror. 'You think I'm loco?' he protested. 'That wire may be cut miles away, and them Sioux could bushwhack us all along the line. I ain't leavin' this town, that's a fact, Marshal.'

'Look, Myron, you and me has a duty to do.'

'Well, I does mine in town. Not out there with them Indians on the loose.'

'You've got the equipment?'

'Sure. Spare wire, insulators, and even a few poles stored back of the office. If you want to go takin' risks with your hair, that's up to you. I aim to hang on to mine until nature takes it away.'

The marshal looked round a little desperately and the man took pity on him.

'Lookit, Marshal,' he said soothingly, 'them wires could have been cut any place, and they probably chopped down the poles to do it. It's a job for a team of men when that happens. You need ladders and a gang of diggers who know what they're doin'. You ain't gettin' no volunteers until it's safe out there.'

They stopped talking as the gun-dealer came across to join them.

'Do you think they're goin' to attack the town?' Sid Welland asked uneasily.

'Not unless there's more of them than we've seen so far,' the marshal assured him. 'I reckon they're just a few wild young fellas gettin' high on corn liquor and out for easy pickings.'

The blacksmith had come up to join the little group. He was the one who had been at the centre of the noisy crowd a few minutes earlier.

'I reckon as how we ought to put an end to that place at Milo Creek,' he said in a loud voice. 'Folks ain't safe if them red devils is free to leave and burn down farms and suchlike.'

There was a murmuring of agreement from everybody within hearing. The marshal waved them back to their positions around the edges of town.

'Keep your eyes open,' he warned them.

They dispersed reluctantly and joined the other men at the barricades.

Only the blacksmith remained. Ned Floyd was a stubborn man, short, but powerfully built with a thick black beard and dark eyes under a mass of unkempt hair.

'What about these fellas?' he asked loudly as he pointed at Sid Welland and Rico.

'What about them?' the marshal asked.

'They been supplyin' them Indians with guns,

47

that's what about. They're the cause of all this trouble.'

The preacher came hurrying across the street. He waved a calming hand and tried to tell the blacksmith that Sid Welland was innocent of any dealings with the Indians at Milo Creek.

'I don't buy that bill of goods,' the blacksmith said roughly. 'This here fella might not have left town, but he sure as hell has been seein' some strange-lookin' folk behind my corral in the early hours of the mornin'.'

They all looked at the storekeeper and his white face told the marshal that the shot had hit home.

'What's this all about, Welland?' he asked tautly.

The gun-dealer eased himself slightly away so that he stood a little behind Rico.

'They've got it all wrong, Marshal,' he said ingratiatingly. 'One of the ranches sent into town for a few guns, and with all that rain we had lately, their wagon was delayed and it got to town late one night. It was only a few rifles.'

Before the marshal could ask any questions, the blacksmith had something more to say.

'It was a full case of Winchesters!' he shouted. 'I could see 'em clear as day. There was at least a dozen guns in that crate.'

Welland swallowed and nodded his head eagerly. 'Yes, yes,' he agreed. 'They come cheaper that way. But they was sold to our own people. I don't supply guns to no Indians.'

'Then you can simply tell us the name of the rancher who bought them,' the preacher said quietly.

'I . . . I've forgotten.'

More townfolk were gathering round now and the Indians on the edge of town seemed almost to have been ignored.

'You don't remember a customer who buys a whole case of Winchesters?' the marshal asked coldly. 'Not many folk round here can afford to buy that many guns at one time.'

Sid Welland looked frantically around for inspiration. Only Rico stood up for him, putting his bulk between the crowd and the frightened man. His hand was on the stock of the rifle that he cradled in his massive arms.

'You gotta have an explanation, Sid,' the marshal insisted.

'I promised not . . . he'll kill me . . . !' the man shouted.

'Who'll kill you?' the preacher asked anxiously.

Sid Welland realized that the threat of a menacing crowd was more certain than that of somebody out of town.

'It was Steve Holby,' he said hurriedly. 'He and two other ranchers are gettin' ready for a show-down over that land near Barton Creek. Steve reckons that he's bein' robbed of water and he aims to drive the Cullen and Smithson lot off the range. He bought fifteen Winchesters and twenty boxes of cartridges from me. He don't want word to get out until it's all over.'

The marshal whistled. 'Twenty cartons! He'll sure do a lotta shootin' with a thousand bullets. We could have quite a range war on our hands if this goes through. Sid, your duty was to report all this business to the law. You ain't got the sense of a jackrabbit.'

'But he's got the greed of one,' the blacksmith laughed. He seemed to have lost his malice now that the Indians were not involved.

The mayor looked uneasily from one to the other. 'Well, it's outside our area, Marshal,' he said, 'and in the meantime we still have these red devils to handle.'

'Judgin' by the lack of shootin', they seem to have left us,' the banker said as he approached with a shotgun in his hand. 'They let out a few whoops and rode over the bluff to the south-west. All the same, they could come back, and in the middle of the night when we're not prepared.'

Marshal Tovey was not taking much notice of the conversation. His eyes were on the Winchester that Rico Edwards was holding across his chest.

'Let's have a look at that gun, Rico,' the lawman said quietly.

The man clutched it tighter. 'Why the hell should I?' he demanded.

'Because I asked nicely. Hand it over.'

Rico looked at his boss but Sid Welland's eyes were on the rifle the man held. He seemed puzzled for a moment before his face suddenly paled as he saw what the marshal had already spotted.

'Now, Marshal . . . !' he began hesitantly.

He was too late as Will Tovey snatched the gun out of Rico's unresisting hand and checked the maker's mark. It was only two numbers different from that of the dead Indian's gun. They had come from the same batch.

'I think you've some explainin' to do, Sid,' the marshal said ominously to the trader. 'And it had better be good.'

'Marshal, I never sold no guns to Indians. I ain't stupid.'

The blacksmith pushed his way forward and grabbed Sid Welland by the lapels of his coat.

'I reckon you're for a hangin', fella,' he snarled. 'Them guns is bein' used against decent folk.'

There was a murmur from the gathering crowd and if there were any Indians still on the outskirts of town, they were almost completely forgotten.

The marshal tried to separate the gun-dealer from the tight grip of the blacksmith. It was not possible and the lawman was also being jostled by the hostile townsfolk who were looking and sounding dangerous.

'I'm takin' Rico and Sid Welland to the jail-house,' the lawman shouted above the noise. He turned to the blacksmith. 'You're deputized, Ned. Make sure they get there safely and lock them in separate cells. I'll be along in a minute.'

Will Tovey's confident manner took the fight out of the smith and he obediently did as ordered. The mob parted to let him and his two charges through. As they passed, the marshal removed Rico's Colt from its holster and stood watching while Ned Floyd pushed his way across the street to enter the jailhouse.

The folk began to disperse uncertainly, edging their way back to the various positions they had previously occupied at the town defences.

The preacher touched the marshal warmly on the arm.

'You pulled off a good one there, Will,' he chuckled. 'Giving the chief troublemaker a deputy's job sure made him forget about a lynching. I really thought it was going to happen for a moment.'

'So did I, and I couldn't have stopped it.'

The preacher shook his head sadly. 'I'm sorry if I misled you about Sid Welland,' he said. 'I really did believe that the Milo Creek Indians had no guns.'

'The funny thing is, Ely,' Will Tovey said, 'that I was inclined to agree with you. But we've seen the guns, and folk always forget that Winchester stamp a number and a letter of the alphabet on each one. I reckon he's been sellin' to the reservation, and I aim to have him up before the travellin' judge for it.'

Will Tovey had a quiet word with the mayor before mounting his horse. He rode to the edge of the main street from where the Indians had last been seen on the distant bluff. There was no sign of movement now as some of the men moved an upturned wagon to let him gallop through. He rode swiftly out on the dusty trail through clumps of stunted bushes and up the long slope of withered grass to where he could get a better view of the area. All he could see was a vague cloud of dust that marked the path the Indians had taken.

The marshal edged round to the left where the telegraph poles formed an irregular line towards the next town. He trotted his animal for a couple of miles without finding any wires down or poles damaged. He turned for home reluctantly, keeping a careful eye out for movement among the low bushes as he went.

There was still a slight smudge of dark smoke away to the south and he tried to remember who lived out in that direction. He would have to investigate sooner or later, but Will Tovey admitted to himself that he was nervous at going so far out of town until the position was a little clearer.

He headed back to Newton Crossing and was in his office an hour later. Everything was back to normal. The streets had been cleared, the children ushered back to the schoolhouse, while people moved around again with expressions of relief on their faces.

The mayor and council held an urgent meeting. Banker Lesser fretted over his money, while the preacher did his best to pacify the more hysterical elderly ladies who automatically rushed to him for assurance that God had not deserted them.

Sid Welland and Rico sat disconsolately on their bunks while Ned Floyd, in his new role as a deputy marshal, sat proudly near the stove with a cup of coffee in his hand and a badge on his waistcoat. He had found it while looking for the cell keys and now wore it with an air of satisfaction.

He poured out some coffee for Will Tovey as the two men settled down to discuss events. They were deep in conversation when an uproar seemed to erupt in the street.

The marshal hurried to the door just in time to see a two-wheeled rig pulled by a single sweating horse career to a halt outside his office. A woman was driving, her grey hair unkempt and free from its pins as she climbed down and tied the reins to the hitching rail. Will Tovey remembered who she was; Mrs Cavetty from a small farm out on the trail to the south. It was from that direction that the haze of smoke had risen. He bit his lip and offered his hand as she mounted the wooden steps.

A crowd was gathering and her voice was loud and angry.

'They've killed my Davy!' she screamed. 'Them red devils have killed my man and burned down our house!'

SIX

An uneasy night had passed. Neighbours had taken in the hysterical woman, while the town council met in their room over the mayor's store. The crowds had gathered on the street, angry now instead of frightened, and the blacksmith had deserted from his deputy's post and was playing a part again as one of the mob-leaders.

The men were armed while the women egged them on to violence against the two men in jail. Mrs Cavetty had seen the people who had burned her home, yelping and shooting wildly as they slaughtered the domestic animals around the farm after throwing burning torches into the barn and the house. They were using Winchesters, waving them proudly as they galloped madly around, killing her husband as he tried to fend off their attack. Mrs Cavetty had hidden in the little store cellar, only emerging when all was quiet and the density of the smoke drove her up for fresh air.

Marshal Tovey was not at the mayoral meeting. He was stuck in the barricaded jailhouse with nobody to help him. The two men in the cells hung anxiously on to the bars, seeing the blazing torches on the street and hearing the menacing noise of the townspeople. The prisoners stayed awake all night, as did the marshal, and only the heavy, iron-bound door and shuttered windows kept the mob from storming the building to drag out their victims for a hanging from the corn-merchant's loading-beam.

Dawn broke with a slight mist and the reek of the dead torches in the still air. The marshal looked out from behind a partly opened shutter. The main street was deserted except for a rat that was scuttling home after a night of foraging. He could hear a few birds singing as the sun tried to struggle through the clouds.

'Well, I reckon you two is lucky,' he said wearily to the two men as they huddled on their bunks. 'They'll be more reasonable this mornin'. A night's sleep kinda brings folks to their senses.'

'They were goin' to lynch us last night,' Sid Welland said hoarsely.

'They might do it yet, but I figure on them as havin' settled down some. The mayor and the preacher calmed them down a bit, but if the hotheads get 'em riled up again, there's still no tellin' what might happen. It's that damned blacksmith we have to reckon with. He's got a hot temper and he fancies himself as some sort of leader. I'll make you breakfast, but don't expect too much. I wasn't reckonin' on company.'

Will Tovey turned to the stove and busied himself with making some fresh coffee while the two men sat miserably behind bars.

'I didn't sell guns to Indians,' Sid Welland said for the umpteenth time.

'So how come one of them was carryin' a new Winchester and Rico had a gun from the same batch?'

There was a long silence as the marshal added some wood to the Imperial stove.

'It weren't Indians.'

'If you say so. But try tellin' that to a lynch mob and see where it gets you.'

There was a knock on the back door of the jail-house and Marshal Tovey unholstered his gun before going down the corridor to see who was there through a crack in the shutter.

It was preacher Thomas, looking very furtive and carrying a covered basket on his arm. The lawman opened the door and pulled him in.

'I've brought some food,' the preacher said breathlessly. 'I figured as how you might not be well stocked up, and couldn't leave the prisoners to go get some.'

'That's right considerate of you, Ely. All I had

was a few eggs and a bit of ham for my own meal.
This is real welcome. What's happenin' in town?'

'The mayor's sent men out in each direction to
try and find the break in the telegraph wires, and
he has young Jimmy Paulus scoutin' around in
case the Indians come back. You've got trouble,
Will. The folks is real scared and they figure on
getting together and raiding the Milo Creek
reservation. They won't listen to the mayor or
me.'

'Well, we can't stop 'em, but if the wire can be
fixed, the army will show up to sort things out
one way or another. I suppose Ned Floyd is
leadin' the trouble?'

The preacher nodded. 'Him and that crowd of
drunks from Ma Bresson's saloon. They're also
keen on lynching your prisoners. I can't make
them see reason.'

Will Tovey nodded moodily. 'Yeah, I reckon
they're mad as hell, and if I leave this place for a
minute, they'll have those two outa here slick as
spit. Sid Welland swears he didn't sell guns to the
Sioux, and I'm almost inclined to believe him.
But they got the guns and they're on the move. If
we can get the army in when the line's repaired,
I'll send them out of town for trial. It's the best I
can do.'

The preacher left a few minutes later while the
marshal supplied his unwilling guests with their
breakfast. He stood watching them make a list-

less meal, washing it down with hot coffee.

'The folks still want to lynch you two,' he said bluntly, 'and there ain't a heap I can do about it once they break in here.'

'I've told you . . .' Sid Welland began.

'I know what you told me but it don't make sense. If you don't get hanged here in town, you'll be taken to the county seat and tried there. Nobody's goin' to believe that you ain't been tradin' with the Milo Creek Indians.'

Rico Edwards got up from his bunk and pressed his face against the bars so that he could catch a glimpse of his boss in the next cell.

'Tell him, for God's sake!' he yelled. 'I don't figure on hangin' for no lousy Winchesters!'

'Shut up, you fool!' Sid Welland shouted back. 'The marshal has to protect us, and they'll have the wire restored today or tomorrow. Once that's done, things will be different. Just keep your head and rely on me.'

'You sure got confidence in me,' Will Tovey grinned. 'But suppose the folk get riled up and break in? Do you expect me to be a hero?'

'It's your job!'

Will Tovey went up to the bars until his face was only a few inches from that of Sid Welland.

'Let me tell you somethin',' he said tightly. 'I don't like the smell of you or your gunhand here. If the folk break into the jailhouse, I'll be standin' aside and lettin' them get on with it. They don't pay me enough to take on a whole town. Just think about that.'

When Preacher Thomas left the jailhouse, he returned to the office of the mayor where a crowd was gathered. The voices of the women were loudest, encouraging the men to enter the building and insist upon action being taken against the reservation. The preacher pushed his way through and entered the sweet-smelling store. It was crowded. Not with customers but with more folk who were trying to intimidate the town council.

Preacher Thomas hurried upstairs into the smoke-filled office of the mayor. The councillors were gathered round his desk, sweating with heat and nervousness. They all looked anxiously at the newcomer as though he might be their saviour.

'What's happening?' he asked them tautly. 'They still seem mighty riled out there.'

'Ned Floyd's taken over,' the mayor said sadly. 'He's got them raidin' Welland's store for extra guns and ammunition. Then they're loadin' up supplies on a couple of wagons and headin' out of town. They're goin' to settle with the Indians once and for all. I can't stop 'em. There's nigh on a hundred involved. Practically every able-bodied man in town is goin' along.'

'Maybe they shouldn't be stopped,' somebody said bluntly.

61

There was a murmur of agreement from the dozen or so people in the room.

'We can't let them go massacring folks,' Ely Thomas protested. 'It isn't human and I reckon we should let the army deal with the matter.'

'That's more or less what I said,' the mayor muttered, 'but the hotheads are takin' over and they're all for killin' Indians.'

There was a roar of applause from the street below and the councillors rushed to the windows to see what was happening. Two wagons had drawn up outside Sid Welland's gun store and the blacksmith was directing the loading of guns and other supplies into them. There was already food and some barrels of beer or water aboard the rigs as more townsmen came back on the scene with their saddled horses while the womenfolk clustered around them, hugging and kissing their heroes.

'Well, at least they've given up the idea of lynching Sid Welland,' the preacher said thankfully.

'Don't be so sure,' the mayor muttered as he watched fearfully. 'What's Wally Finlay carrying?'

The town drunk was hurrying across the street with a length of rope in his hands. A cheer went up as someone threw the end of it over the loading-beam of one of the stores.

'We have to do something,' Preacher Thomas said desperately. 'We can't let this happen.'

Nobody spoke as the mayor walked slowly back to his desk to take up his glass of whiskey again.

'There's too many of them,' he said flatly. 'Maybe the marshal . . .'

'He's on his own in that jailhouse. They'll break in and drag those men out to their deaths. The marshal may even get killed himself. We've got to go down there and stop them.'

The preacher looked round the room but nobody answered him. The town council were better at talking than at doing, and none of them liked the sound of the noise coming from the street below.

Ely Thomas did not think himself a brave man, but he had a keen sense of duty and left the cowering elders of the town to go and see if he could help the marshal. He pushed his way through the noisy crowd and confronted the little group who were leading them.

'What is all this nonsense?' he demanded. 'You are acting like a bunch of savages instead of decent, Christian folk. You, Tom Williams, and you, Marcus Holmes, have you any idea how silly you seem with those guns and the wild looks on your faces? Now get off home and tend your business. The marshal knows his duty and he's doing it right fine.'

He thought for a moment that he had made an impression, but it was the blacksmith who pushed forward and stood like a belligerent bull in front of the fat little cleric.

'Keep out of this,' Ned Floyd said menacingly. 'We aim to deal with them murderin' red fellas and those who've been sellin' them guns. You go tend your bible readin' and leave the peace-keepin' to those as knows how.'

The spell was broken and the crowd howled like a multi-headed demon as it followed the blacksmith towards the jailhouse and left the preacher standing in the middle of the dusty street. The little man hurried after them and reached the porch outside the marshal's office a few steps ahead of the angry mob. He spread out his hands in a gesture of pacifying calmness.

'Friends!' he shouted, but someone pushed him aside and half a dozen men tried to break into the building. The sturdy door held but the glass of the windows was shattered by the butts of guns that then pounded on the shutters behind them. Some of the men ran round to the rear of the jail-house to smash a hitching rail and use it as a battering ram against the back door.

It was this that gave way first. The hinges burst and the heavy wooden panels caved in to fling the angry group of men into the passageway that led to the cells and the front of the building. One of them ran across the office and slid the bolts on the front door. The rest of the mob piled in, led by the blacksmith who wielded a large hammer.

There was a moment of silence as they all stood in the marshal's office. Somebody opened the shutters to let in a little more light and every eye was directed to the cells at the rear. They were empty.

SEVEN

It was a disappointed mob that set out for Milo Creek. They had gone round to the corral at the rear of the jailhouse to find that the horses were also missing. Marshal Tovey appeared to have released his prisoners or taken them out of town for safety. The town drunk threw down the rope in disgust, while those who were more sober gathered round the blacksmith for their orders about killing every Indian they came across.

The ride was a long one, stopping the first night by a muddy stream where they quarrelled over the shortage of drinkable water. The barrels they had brought along contained beer, and not everybody was happy with that arrangement. Heads were beginning to cool with the chill of the evening and Ned Floyd was not as popular as he had been earlier in the day.

They set out again at dawn, a group of nearly

a hundred heavily armed townsmen who were becoming less belligerent with every mile they travelled. The sun poured down an unrelenting heat and it was late afternoon when they reached Jesse Parker's small farm. His Indian wife was sitting at the door of the house, her hands busy with husks of corn and she looked at the approaching horde with a blank, unreadable expression.

Ned Floyd pushed his horse forward to take up his diminishing authority again.

'Where's that Indian-lovin' husband of yours?' he asked in a loud voice. The woman rose from her stool as the corn spilled from the enamel bowl. She hurried into the house just as Jesse was emerging with a shotgun in his hands.

'What the hell is all this?' he demanded angrily. 'Are you folk ridin' off to war or something?'

'We're ridin' to Milo Creek to finish off them Indian friends of your'n!' Ned Floyd shouted. 'They've done their last thievin' and killin' of decent folk!'

There was a loud murmur of agreement as Jesse Parker stepped forward.

'Now, just you listen to me, Ned Floyd,' he said peaceably. 'Them Indians didn't do no harm to nobody. I just got back from there and I was comin' into town to have a word with the marshal.'

'You're practically one of them yo'self!' somebody shouted.

There was a chorus of approval as old Jesse licked his pale lips and stepped forward with one hand raised so that he might be heard.

'We don't want no Indian-lovers in this territory!' Ned Floyd shouted in case any of the others usurped his leadership. He drew his pistol and fired a single shot.

It took the old man in the chest and he staggered backwards, the shotgun falling from his grasp as he slumped across the open doorway. His wife dragged him inside and slammed the door shut. There was a howl of derision as they heard her barring it against an attack. A few shots were fired at the house while the horses pawed the ground nervously at the noise.

It was Ned Floyd who again took charge.

'Burn 'em out!' he shouted.

Some of the mob dismounted to start hammering on the shutters of the little house. Torches were made and thrown up on the roof while two of the men piled wood against the door and set it alight. A few remained on their horses, a little ashamed at what was happening but afraid to look too friendly towards the injured old man and his wife.

A shot burst from behind the shutters. It was a blast from a scatter-gun and caught one of the fire lighters full in the face. He reeled backwards in a shower of blood while the others hurriedly ran for their horses before Ned Floyd could issue any orders. The riders disappeared in a cloud of grey dust while the farmhouse began to burn fiercely.

There was another day of hard riding to reach Milo Creek. The sun poured down hotly as they travelled, while a keen wind came off the distant hills to throw sudden chills at their sweaty bodies. Some of the older men were regretting their decision to ride with the mob. What had happened at Jesse Parker's farm was weighing heavily on them as they got further from home. Ned Floyd was also losing his nerve. Being a leader was different from what he had imagined. The longer they travelled, the harder it was to keep the riders from quarrelling and grumbling.

It was dusk when they reached the head of the creek that sent its stream of clear, cold water through the wide, well-grassed valley which led to the reservation. He called a halt for a rest and there was an immediate objection to his command.

'Let's get 'em before the night sets in!' one of the men shouted angrily.

Others bawled their agreement and it was some minutes before Ned Floyd could make himself heard.

'Now, listen to me,' he said as he looked round

the cluster of horsemen. 'We rest up here until just before dawn. Our horses need it, and I reckon we do as well. We have a meal, a few hours sleep, and then we go in just as daylight is breakin' and we can see what we're doin'. We take them before they wakes, and we slaughter the lot.'

'What about that preacherman they got, Ned?' somebody asked. 'Ain't he the government agent?'

Ned Floyd grinned. 'He sure as hell is,' he agreed, 'and I reckon he must know all that them Indians was doin'. So if he catches a stray bullet, who's to worry?'

'We could be in trouble over this,' somebody said fearfully. 'We're a territory now and there's a legislature.'

'And what in hell has this legislature done to protect decent folk?' Ned Floyd snarled. 'We get raided and burned out by Indians and see money spent on keepin' 'em clothed and fed in reservations. We got rights too, and no government fellas is worryin' their crooked heads off about it. They're all too busy tellin' us to love them red devils.'

He got a murmur of agreement from most of the men and they gradually settled down to eat and sleep.

They awoke before dawn, washed hurriedly in the bitterly cold creek, ate a quick meal, and then saddled up their mounts to troop slowly into the valley as the stars paled and a very faint sign of daylight crept across the bare hills.

They halted after a couple of hours, dismounting for a rest while Ned Floyd and a few others rode ahead to breast a small hill so that they could look down on the winding stream with the Indian reservation spreading out on either side of it. The lightening of the sky showed the sharp outlines of several dozen small huts amid an assortment of tents. Hobbled horses wandered aimlessly and slowly around the area while a few dogs moved in the trampled grass as they looked for a morning meal. It was too early for human beings to be around, and no smoke came from any of the dwellings.

There was one larger shack built of stout logs that supported a turf roof. It had a stone chimney at one end with a pile of freshly cut timber stored close by. There was a corral alongside with two horses poking their heads across the rail while the Union flag hung limply from a tall pole a few yards away.

'They sure ain't early risers,' chuckled Ned Floyd as he viewed the scene. 'I reckon we have just to get ourselves down there and shoot every damned thing that moves. Don't give 'em a chance to kill any more folks.'

One of the men urged his horse forward. 'Suppose we run off their animals,' he said eagerly. 'They might get away on them.'

'Hell, no. They're hobbled and it would take too much time. And give them too much warning.'

Ned Floyd looked around as he sized up the ground.

'I reckon we come in from this point. Straight down the slope and in among the tents. Then the cabins. And don't forget that we kill everybody. No witnesses to carry tales to them territory fellas. Now, let's go bring up the rest of them and get it all over with.'

They turned their mounts back to rejoin the rest of the waiting townsmen. A few of the riders had already eyed the Indian horses with interest. There were also some animal hides drying on frames that would bring a good market price in town. There could be some rich pickings when the killing was done.

They were in position a quarter of an hour later, looking down the grassy slope as they waited for Ned Floyd to give the signal. The sun was above the hills now, throwing long shadows and dissolving the mist that was rising from the dewy ground. A dog barked at the sight of the long line of riders stretched across the top of the ridge, but it was the only warning the Indians got as Ned raised a hand to signal the charge.

No imposed discipline could stop the yells of the men as they rode their horses among the tents, firing at every human being emerging into

the sunlight. They circled amid an uproar of
barking dogs, screams of women and children,
and the rapid explosions of Colts, shotguns, and
Winchesters.

The Indians struggled as best they could, stag-
gering into the sunlight with old Springfield
rifles that they fumbled with clumsily. Some had
bows and arrows but were shot down before they
loosed off more than a few shafts. A woman ran
towards the Indian agent's office but was brought
down with a shotgun blast before she had gone
twenty yards. She collapsed at the closed door,
reaching vainly for the help she thought was in
the building.

Ned Floyd paused amid the confusion to reload
his Colt .44 while he looked around at what was
happening. Some of the cabins were alight while
a few of his followers were urging their mounts to
trample down the tents around the inhabitants.
He could see only one of his men unhorsed and
injured. It was the Indians who had taken the
worst of things as corpses began to litter the
bloody ground.

The blacksmith dismounted outside the Indian
agent's cabin and pushed at the stout door. It
opened to his touch and he hesitated for a
moment before entering. He gave the door a
sharp kick, and then leapt forward, gun ready for
use. To his surprise, the Indian agent was only
just rising from his bed; an elderly, pale-faced

man in a thick woollen nightshirt, and with legs bare and shaky.

Ned Floyd fired one shot. It took the elderly preacher in the chest and he fell backwards on to the bed. He hardly moved again as the blacksmith searched the cabin for whatever valuables there were.

When he stepped back into the daylight, it was all over. The Indians were dead or lying wounded amid the wreckage of their homes. Ned's own followers were staring around as if amazed at what they had done.

'They hardly put up a fight,' one of the men said in wonder. 'I always reckoned as how the Sioux was tough. We sure beat the hell out of them, Ned. Jeff Cain's the only one hurt, and he'll survive if he stays away from doctors.'

Ned Floyd grinned. 'That's generalship,' he said proudly. 'We took 'em by surprise and they was so shook that they never stood a chance. I figure as how we've scored one for General Custer. The folks back home will surely be relieved when we tell them what happened here. They can sleep peaceable in their beds now.'

There was a strange silence from most of the men. Some still sat on their horses, looking a little shocked while others went among the carnage to loot whatever they could find. There was food in plenty; hides and saddles, and blankets that were still bloodstained. Silver

ornaments were ripped from the dead and dying
to be stuffed into the pockets of the raiders. Some
of the men entered the Indian agent's storeroom
despite the feeble protests of the blacksmith.

'Them's government stores in there!' he
shouted as they began to loot the place. 'We can't
go stealin' from the government.'

'Why not?' one of them shouted back. 'They
steal from us.'

Ned Floyd was ignored as the men tramped in
and out across the body of the dead Indian
woman and past the corpse of the preacher. They
loaded themselves with more blankets, medi-
cines, and cooking utensils. Floyd had lost control
and watched helplessly as they fired the cabin
and led their laden mounts back to where the
wagons were waiting.

All that they left behind them was a desolated
patchwork of smoke and flame, with sprawling
bodies over which the buzzards were already
gathering.

EIGHT

Marshal Tovey had not left town with his prisoners. He had simply taken them out through the rear door while the mob was arguing on the street. He had shepherded the two men into the corral to gather three horses, and then ordered them to take the animals to a nearby grain warehouse where they sheltered until the irate citizens had left Newton Crossing.

When the place was quiet again and only the dust of the departing horses was left to disturb the air, they came out from the warehouse and went back to the marshal's office. He ushered his two prisoners back into their cells before crossing the street to have a talk with a distraught mayor and council.

They were glad to see their lawman as all gathered round the big desk in Bob Harris's office.

'I don't like this,' the mayor said miserably. 'We've got the whole town breakin' the law and there's nothin' we can do about it. If they kill them Indians, the government will call it plain murder and they'll look to me and you, Marshal, as the ones who should have stopped it.'

Will Tovey nodded absent-mindedly. He was thinking of something else.

The banker coughed to draw attention to himself.

'What happened to you and your prisoners, Will?' he asked.

The lawman told him and received a murmur of approval from the assembled councillors.

'So what do we do now?' the mayor asked in a distracted voice.

'I suggest that we release Sid Welland and Rico,' the preacher said bluntly.

There was a chorus of dissent but Marshal Tovey nodded his agreement.

'I'm inclined to believe Welland,' he said. 'Some of the ranchers are headin' up for a range war over water rights. The Winchesters are what they'd need instead of those old things they go totin' around like family relics. There's also another point to be considered.' He turned to the banker. 'Did Sid Welland pay any big sums of money into the bank lately?'

Frank Lesser hesitated for a moment. He was a discreet man and well thought of in the town.

'I don't like to discuss a man's affairs,' he protested.

'It may be in Welland's best interests if you do,' the marshal insisted.

'Well, he did pay in a large sum. We were rather surprised.'

'The sort of money a bunch of Indians would have?'

There was a long pause as the situation dawned on the men around the desk. Their faces lightened to some degree.

'Lord bless you, no,' the banker chuckled. 'Indians could never have that sort of money. I see what you mean now, Marshal.'

Will Tovey stood up to look out of the steamy window. The street was almost deserted save for a few women, a stray dog, and running children who had been let out of the schoolroom. A steady breeze blew up little wisps of dust while the store signs creaked noisily.

'We gotta treat Sid Welland careful-like,' the marshal said softly. 'His store has been broken into; goods stolen; he's been put in jail, and I reckon he must feel that he has a real case for compensation. He's mighty mad at us, but at least I was able to save him from a lynchin'. I hope he remembers that when he takes us all to court.'

'You'd better let him go,' the mayor said nervously. 'I'll come across with you and try and smooth things over. He might be reasonable.'

Judging from the expression on Sid Welland's face as he sat in the jailhouse cell, reasonable was not the word to be used. He jumped up as the door opened to admit the marshal and the bustling little mayor.

'I want out of here!' he shouted. 'I got rights, and you've let that mob loot my store!'

He broke off as the lawman took the keys down from the hook and opened the barred door.

'Don't get too excited, Sid,' he warned the gun-dealer. 'You sold guns to folks who are aimin' to start a range war. Now, that ain't neighbourly, and you gotta admit that I saved you from a hangin' back there. You've been put away in this nice, safe jailhouse to keep you from swingin' delicate-like from the grain-store loadin'-beam. Be a little grateful, Sid. I done saved your life.'

The two men emerged, Rico towering over his boss as they stood before the marshal's desk.

'That's all very well,' the dealer snapped, 'but what about my business? It could be ruined.'

'Look at it this way, Sid,' the mayor said in a persuasive voice. 'You've been sellin' guns to ranchers who could cause this town some almighty trouble. A judge wouldn't like that if we made a complaint about it all official-like. Then again, that mob will be back in three or four days with all your rifles intact. You'll get them back good as new, and I'll see that the bullets are paid for. So you won't suffer too much, will you? Not as much as them poor Indians.'

'I don't give a horse's ass about no Indians!' the storekeeper yelled. 'But I reckon more than guns and ammunition have been stolen from my place. I could be thousands of dollars adrift there. I aim to take you and the marshal before the courts and get what's due to me.'

'You do that little thing, Sid,' the marshal said dryly, 'and you might really get what's due to you.'

'Are you threatenin' me?'

The mayor pushed between the lawman and the angry arms-dealer.

'Take it easy, fellas,' he urged. 'Just let's wait patiently and see what happens when the folks get back to town.'

Sid Welland was going to say something else when the door of the jailhouse burst open. Three men pushed into the office, their clothes covered with trail dust and their unshaven faces red with sun and scouring winds. They carried shotguns in their gloved hands and the weapons pointed unerringly at the four men who stood gaping in surprise at the sight.

Nine

Sid Welland let out an audible gasp while the belligerent Rico made a sound like the snarl of an animal. He found a shotgun barrel pressed into his stomach and halted in his tracks. It was the mayor who went for the small pistol under his coat. It was in his hand and already cocked before he was hit in the face with the butt of one of the guns. He staggered backwards against the cell bars, his mouth streaming blood as he dropped the weapon.

Will Tovey said nothing. He simply awaited events while the intruders looked carefully around before locking their captives in the cells.

No words had been spoken until the keys were placed on the desk next to their guns. The biggest of the men was youngish, with a long face and heavy jaw. He grinned at his prisoners as he removed the bottle of whiskey from the little cupboard and took a swig from it before passing it to his companions.

'Now, I'll tell you how it is, folks,' he said in a friendly voice, 'you just keep yourselves quiet here, and we'll be out of town again before you know what's happened. Ain't no point in gettin' uppity or makin' a fuss. Our business in your fair city will be over fast as fast, so just rest easy and nobody gets hurt.'

'I take it that you're stealin' somethin'?' the marshal asked in a mild voice.

'You got it right there, lawman,' the tall fellow grinned. 'We aim to loot this little town from one end to the other. You got a fine bank here and some good stores, and we're goin' to empty them all. Food, dry goods, saddles, guns, and all them lovely dollars.'

'While everyone's away killin' Indians,' Will Tovey muttered.

All three of their captors burst into laughter.

'You're sure smart, Marshal,' one of the others said. 'We got you so riled up at them Indians that the folk damn near emptied this town to go a-killin'. Now, ain't that the way to do a little robbin'?'

There was more laughter as the stout mayor struggled from his seat on the narrow bunk and pushed Rico out of the way to stand at the bars of the cell.

'But you're causin' a massacre!' he shouted at them. 'Innocent women and children are bein' slaughtered because of this!'

The tall man moved closer to the cells.

'They're only Indians,' he said cheerfully, 'and I don't reckon much loss to anybody. We got this town sewn up tight, fella. And we're takin' every cent you folks have got. Startin' with the bank.'

'You're not touchin' my store!' Sid Welland shouted with sudden courage. 'You can't do that! We . . . .'

He broke off and licked his lips uneasily. It was Will Tovey who broke the slight silence that followed.

'They've planned this well, Mr Mayor,' he said calmly. 'All them Indians hoverin' round the town weren't Indians at all. They was this gang of coyotes. They burned folk out, created a panic, cut the telegraph, and just waited until the people got riled enough and scared enough to go wipe out the reservation at Milo Creek.'

'You hit it in one, fella,' the tall man agreed. 'There ain't a dozen fightin' men left in the town and we took 'em all by surprise. We got this place to ourselves, so you just sit quiet while we go make us a few dollars.'

He headed for the door, followed by the other two. All three were grinning broadly as they passed through to the street. Will Tovey took a look at the injured mayor and realized that apart from a cut mouth and two damaged teeth, he had got off lightly. It was Sid Welland who looked more desperate. He was chewing his lip while his hands restlessly tore at the lapels of his coat.

'You seem real worried, Sid,' the marshal said quietly.

'Worried! Of course I'm worried. They'll take everything I've got. Stock, money . . . !'

'Well, the townsfolk have some of your weapons and you're in the same pickle-barrel as every other storekeeper in town. Could be worse. You're still alive, at least.'

'But they pro . . . !'

He sat down next to the mayor while Rico went to the little barred window that overlooked the rear of the jailhouse. He tested the ironwork and grunted in disappointment.

'Don't waste your time there,' the marshal told him. 'This is a mighty secure place. We're here until somebody lets us out.'

'Or kills us,' moaned Sid Welland.

The mayor shook his head in despair.

'I don't understand all this,' he moaned as he held a bandanna to his mouth and nose.

'We've been took,' Will Tovey told him bluntly. 'These fellas have planned it all very careful-like and we fell into the trap like a bunch of rubes. The town's wide open to them.'

'My God! I wonder what will happen now!'

The town had been taken completely by surprise. After the noise and upset of the vengeful departure, most people had gone back to their homes.

Some were a little ashamed of what had happened, while the children, freed again from the tyranny of education, had gone to play among the corrals and sheds where everything was now strangely quiet.

Myron Davis returned to the telegraph office; the banker went to his imposing brick-built place of business, while the store-owners opened their doors again hoping that somebody might be in the buying mood. The Reverend Ely Thomas shook his head at it all, murmured a few prayers, and scurried along to the wooden church where he sat on a pew, despairing of human nature.

The bandits entered Newton Crossing on all sides. There were twelve of them, no longer disguised as Indians, but all heavily armed, heading for the places where money was to be had. After securing the marshal, the bank was their first target. Three of them burst in to startle staff and customers with levelled guns as they demanded all the cash to be handed over.

Frank Lesser heard the disturbance and came out of his office to find himself covered by shotguns and carbines. He did not pretend to be a brave man, and with staff and a couple of customers to consider, he merely stood aside and watched as the robbers emptied the safe, the cash drawers, and the pockets of everyone in sight.

One man dominated the scene. He was tall and

well built, in his fifties, with rather long hair that brushed against the greasy collar of his dark trail-coat. He had a straggling black moustache that merged into the unshaven area around his chin, and as he stood in front of the open door of the large safe, his startlingly white teeth showed in a broad grin.

'You got one hell of a good bank in this town,' he said in a slightly southern accent. 'Let's hope your storekeepers still have a bit put by at home.'

He watched as his men stuffed the money into large canvas sacks. When it was done, the robbers casually left the building to join their comrades who were already holding up the local stores. Not a shot had been fired as they went from place to place, demanding all the ready cash on threats of burning down the buildings. Without someone to lead them, even the few able-bodied men who were still left in Newton Crossing were reluctant to make any move.

A horse and cart were produced from somewhere and the gang loaded stock from the various stores on to the vehicle. Sid Welland's gun supply was depleted even further as weapons, ammunition, and boxes of blasting-powder were shoved aboard.

Doctor Earle stood on the corner of one of the side-streets. He watched in frustrated anger as the pillaging continued. His wife joined him for a moment but he pushed her back out of sight because she was wearing a gold locket and a silver fob-watch.

The Reverend Ely Thomas was the bravest man in town. He accosted the tall leader of the gang by approaching and grabbing one coated arm. The man turned, listened for a moment to whatever the preacher was saying, and then struck him across the face with a casual blow that sent the little man reeling to his knees. There was laughter from the gang who were now beginning to mount up. One of the saloon girls ran to the aid of Mr Thomas and helped him back to his little house.

With all his men mounted, the gang leader fired a couple of jubilant shots into the air before leading them off at a gallop. A cloud of dust rose several feet high as the cavalcade vanished from sight in the direction of the southern range of hills. The town fell silent while the dust settled again.

After a very humiliated Will Tovey had been released from his own jailhouse, there was a meeting in his office. The stove had been lit, coffee made, and the mayor, a few councillors, and the doctor stood or sat around smoking in the steamy atmosphere. A few of the townspeople looked at them through the windows while other folks checked on their properties to see what had been left after the raid. The bank-manager was missing. He was still totting up the amount of money that had been taken.

It was half an hour before he put in an appearance, his face pale as he clutched a sheet of paper in his chubby hand.

'Twenty-seven thousand dollars,' he said despairingly. 'They couldn't have picked a worse time of the year.'

'How come you was carryin' so much?' Will Tovey asked as he tried not to grin at the discomfiture of the money-lender.

'The local ranchers have just had their money for the cattle sales. They get paid out in cash so that they can use some of it for wages. Then the rest is brought in to us and it was all due to go in to head office next week. We held back the cash because the timber-mills also pay out at this time of the month and they'd have been sending in for some ready cash any day now. I don't know what head office will have to say about this, but I reckon I'll be looking for a new job very shortly.'

The mayor shook his head sadly. 'It wasn't your fault, Frank,' he said. 'It all seems to have been carefully planned. This gang got all the fightin' men out of town before they raided us. Ain't that right, Marshal?'

'It sure is,' Will Tovey agreed, 'and they cut the telegraph, faked all them Indian raids, and were well informed on every move we made. Now then, did anyone recognize any of them?'

There was a general shaking of heads.

'No, and neither did I,' the marshal said regretfully. 'I'd make a guess though that it's a fella who goes by the name of Harry Larrimer. He seems the right age and height and he was an officer in the Confederate army. This affair shows a sort of military plannin' and smacks of a soldier-boy. He specialized in banks down in Wyoming, so I reckon he's made things too hot there and is tryin' his luck further north.'

'Well, he showed more knowledge of tactics than most of the generals I came across,' the doctor said dryly.

There was a silent ripple of nervous laughter before the mayor held up a hand for silence.

'Now, we got a real bad problem on our hands,' he said. 'The town has been raided, there's goin' to be hell to pay if them poor Indians at Milo Creek are harmed, and we ain't got contact with any outside law until the telegraph is fixed. So, what do we do next?'

Everybody looked at the marshal.

'Well, now that we know our trouble wasn't caused by Indians,' he said, 'we can send out wagons and a work-gang led by Myron Davis. He can find out where the trouble is and do a repair job on the wire. The quicker that's done, the quicker we can get in touch with somebody nearer Milo Creek, and the quicker we can get some law after them raiders. We certainly can't chase them ourselves. We just haven't the fire-power.'

'I agree,' said the mayor. 'I'll go have a word with Myron right away.'

'Not afore I fix your face,' the doctor inter-vened. 'You look like you was kicked by a mule. I'd better have a look at Ely Thomas while I'm at it. He took quite a hiding back there.'

They automatically looked round the office, and for the first time, realized that the clergyman was missing.

'Where in hell is he?' the mayor asked.

It was not until they got outside that one of the townsfolk told them that the little preacher had mounted a horse and followed the raiders at a discreet distance.

Ten

The Reverend Ely Thomas was not meant by nature to be riding horses. He was stout, with short legs, and his tiny, delicate hands were not really strong enough to cope with any wilful antics the large bay gelding might try on an inexperienced horseman.

The raiders had not bothered him. Preachers were not rich enough to plunder and he was left alone to go to the livery stable and saddle the first horse he could find. He led it round to his little wooden house, persuaded his reluctant wife to make him up a bag of food, and then he waited by the corner of the main street until the gang mounted up with their stolen money and goods to head out of Newton Crossing.

They travelled at a steady pace, slowed down by the heavily laden cart, and headed straight for the wooded area towards the southern hills, which still bore slight patches of snow.

91

It was easy to follow them. They created a long ribbon of dust until they turned off to the west a little, moving on deep grass that lay flattened by their passing. The little preacher struggled on, gradually getting used to the large horse and the fact that he had not tightened the girth enough and the saddle kept slipping.

He was glad when dusk fell and the group ahead moved off the line of travel to camp for the night at the side of a stream. He could see them light a fire as he sat in the cold darkness and watched with envy as they drank hot coffee and warmed themselves before the cheerful blaze.

They eventually slept and he did the same, dozing fitfully as it got colder. He awoke before they did, ate a little of the cold bacon on a slab of rye bread, and took a swig from the flask of strong ale that his wife had handed him as he left the house. He did not really like alcohol, but it was only the taste and not any temperance attitudes that governed his judgement. It was a safer drink than any local water he might find.

The gang set off again after a while, moving slowly over the more difficult ground that led upwards towards the tree-line. The preacher had to keep well behind, allowing them to get out of sight for long periods when there was no cover of trees or bushes. He feared losing them at times but they were not trying to cover their trail as they moved towards the dense mass of conifers

that lay between them and the range of jagged
hills.

When they disappeared into the tall trees,
Preacher Thomas pulled up his horse and sat
pondering the situation for a while. He was
scared and alone as he slowly dismounted and
led his animal towards the forest.

There was a trail, wide enough for the passage
of the gang's cart with its heavy burden of looted
goods. He followed quietly, listening for the
slightest sound ahead of him.

Ferns grew beneath his feet and a few crea-
tures moved among the tall trunks of the
unfriendly conifers. Here and there another
species of tree had pushed through, rising and
spreading its greener branches and encouraging
a few birds that were already disturbed by the
passage of the gang.

The trees began to thin out and the scene lightened as ahead lay a clearing which backed on to
a long, stony slope of grey rocks where sprouted
clusters of bushes. The hills lay beyond, barren,
and with snow on their upper slopes. Ely Thomas
halted beneath the shelter of a tall pine and
looked at the large, low log-cabin at the back of
the clearing.

It was a solid building with a chimney-breast
at each end. There were crude windows, without
glass but covered with thin sheets of hessian. At
the back of the cabin was a large corral and the

horses were already there, unsaddled to feed from large heaps of freshly cut fodder. The cart lay in front of the cabin door, its load being carried in by several of the gang.

There was smoke from one of the chimneys with a faint smell of cooked bacon wafting on the light air. Ely Thomas made a careful note of everything around before quietly leading his horse back into the wood and going down the trail to the open land beyond.

He remounted, took accurate bearings, and hurried back to Newton Crossing.

The town was in a state of despair. The bank and most of the stores were without money and closed until things could be sorted out in some way. The majority of able-bodied men were away at Milo Creek, and the telegraph was still not working.

Mayor Harris held a public meeting at which he told the assembled people that the raiders were responsible for the troubles blamed on the reservation Indians. They listened in shamed horror. Most of them were the women who had encouraged their men to set out on the murderous expedition. The mayor did not spare them his contempt. While he spoke, the marshal stood quietly, watching the faces of the crowd as he considered his own position.

As they all trooped disconsolately from the church hall, Will Tovey, the mayor, and the banker stayed behind in the porch; a little group of worried men.

'What are we goin' to do about Sid Welland?' Will Tovey asked to nobody in particular.

'What do you mean?' Frank Lesser threw back at him. 'We've agreed that he didn't sell guns to the Indians.'

'True, but I came across one dead Indian with a new Winchester. And he certainly sold them to somebody. I think he supplied the gang that looted the town. It's always possible that they used a few renegade Indians to help create the atmosphere. Gave them guns and whiskey for their help. Welland also let somethin' slip while we was locked up in that jailhouse.'

'What was that?' asked the mayor.

'Remember when I said that we was all in the same pickle-barrel? Sid Welland seemed to think that his store shouldn't have been robbed. He got right agitated when that fella told us they were takin' guns as well as money. Sid actually started to say somethin'. It sounded like, "but they promised", then he clammed up before finishin' it. He'd been quite calm until his affairs were in danger, and it set me wonderin'.'

The banker nodded slowly. 'And you figure he might have sold guns to the raiders and had a deal with them that his store would be left alone?'

'Somethin' like that. And if that gang had three

or four genuine Indians with them, it would certainly account for nearly everything.'

The mayor straightened his back as a gesture of determination.

'I reckon as how we need another talk with Sid Welland,' he said.

Will Tovey shook his head. 'Not yet,' he said firmly. 'I'll send young Ben Wyman out to Steve Holby's spread. He can make it there and back in a day. I'll give the lad a note for Steve and see what he says about buyin' guns from Welland.'

'Do you think he'll admit to startin' a range war?' the mayor asked doubtfully.

'I'll explain the position. I don't think he'll let us down under the circumstances. Do you?'

The mayor thought it over for a moment. 'I reckon not,' he agreed. 'I think we can trust his answer.'

The marshal went off to find the young lad who would make the journey. He also intended to press three of the older townsmen into service to help repair the telegraph line.

The problem there was that Myron Davis was the only one who could do the actual repair, and the wires appeared to be down on both sides of town. All they could do was to travel down the trail towards Fort Preece, do whatever work was needed there, and then come all the way back to move in the opposite direction to repair the line that connected them with Platte Bridge. It was

the Fort Preece connection that was more important and the total line covered a distance of forty
miles.

Myron Davis helped his three assistants to
load the wagon. He looked miserable at the
prospect of a long, hard drive.

The marshal retired to the privacy of his own
office. The raiders had taken all the guns from
his cabinet and a good portion of the more popular calibres of ammunition. The only decent
revolver he had left was an old Colt .45 that he
kept by his bed and a percussion shotgun that no
self-respecting raider would consider stealing. He
looked at the empty spaces in mounting anger
before putting on the coffee-jug and set about
clearing up the mess that had been left.

It was at this point that Myron Davis came
rushing into the jailhouse. His thin face was
more cheerful as he delivered the news.

'The line's back on, Marshal,' he said happily. 'I
just got a message through from Fort Preece. The
soldier-boys must have fixed it.'

'Well, that's good news, Myron, but you still
have to repair the line with Platte Bridge.'

'Maybe the folk at that end will do the work,'
the operator said hopefully as he ran a sweaty
hand through his thick red hair.

'I hope so for your sake, but before you set out,
I've got a long message for the fort. Go tell the
others to start off for Platte Bridge, and then wait

for me to write out the message. You can follow them on horseback when you've sent it through.'

'I already gave the fort an outline,' Myron said eagerly, 'but I didn't think it my place to say too much. After all, the folks here was protectin' themselves.'

'If they've done what they set out to do, a lot of poor souls will be dead by now. I gotta report everythin' that's happened, so wait for me in your office.'

The telegraph operator saw the look on the lawman's face and left the jailhouse without any further argument. Will Tovey wrote out a full description of everything that had happened and took it along to the telegraph office. He stood at the man's shoulder while the key rattled urgently over the forty miles of line. When it was all over, the marshal walked slowly back to his familiar surroundings and made the coffee. All he could do now was to wait.

Young Ben Wyman got back into town around noon the next day. He was covered in dust, his horse lathered with sweat, but he wore the satisfied expression of a man who has made good time and completed his mission. He handed the rancher's note to Marshal Tovey and the lawman thanked and dismissed him before opening it.

It was a short missive, written in stilted pencil,

but it said in quite blunt terms that the only thing the rancher had ever bought from Sid Welland was a shotgun three years ago.

Eleven

The few people on the dusty street watched curiously as the marshal crossed from his office to Sid Welland's gun-store. The dealer was behind the long counter, fitting a new stock to an ancient shotgun that bore traces of rust. He looked up nervously as the lawman entered.

'Look at the place, Marshal,' he complained. 'They've taken all my good stuff. Colts, Remingtons, the good shotguns, and most of my ammunition. There must be the best part of a couple of thousand dollarsworth gone. Between those raiders and the townsfolk, I'm well nigh ruined.'

'I reckon you are at that, Sid,' Will Tovey grinned. 'You wasn't expectin' the gang to steal from your store, was you?'

The man looked at the marshal silently for a moment.

'What do you mean?' he managed to ask.

'Well, you said somethin' in the jailhouse about them promisin' somethin'. I reckon that meant that after you supplied them new guns for the raid, they'd be good enough to leave your place alone. That was the arrangement, wasn't it?'

Sid Welland gave a sickly grin. 'You know me better than that, Will,' he said in a slightly trembling voice. 'I never supplied no Winchesters to anybody but Steve Holby.'

'I just had word from him. He gives you the lie.'

'Well . . . he would, wouldn't he? He ain't goin' to admit to startin' a range war.'

"I'll tell you somethin' else, Sid. You get yourself and Rico Edwards out of this town within the next twenty-four hours or I'm goin' to throw you both back in jail and let the travellin' judge decide what to do about it.'

'I've done nothin' illegal!' the man protested. 'If somebody wants to buy guns and they ain't Indian or drunk, I gotta right to supply. That's the law, Marshal.'

'So you're quotin' law at me now, are you? Well, let me put it another way, Sid. When folks hear that you had a deal goin' with them raiders, they're goin' to get real mad at you. I reckon it could be lynchin' mad. And I'll leave town while they're doin' it.'

The shotgun clattered on to the counter as the dealer reacted to the marshal's words.

'You can't let them . . .'

Before anything else could be said, the door at the end of the store opened and Rico stood there, scruffy and belligerent as he cradled a shotgun in his massive arms. The marshal reached instinctively for the Colt at his belt.

'I ain't for shootin' at nobody,' the big man said in a surprisingly quiet voice. 'I'm leavin' town all peaceable, Marshal. I just wants the pay what's due to me.'

'You can't leave me, Rico!' Sid Welland yelped. 'I need you here.'

'I heard you and the marshal talkin' back there, and I'm just the hired help. That's what you keeps tellin' me, Mr Welland. I don't aim to get myself lynched for your doings. Just pay me off and I'm away. That's fair, ain't it, Marshal?'

Will Tovey nodded. 'I reckon so,' he said cheerfully.

'But I've got no money,' the gun-dealer stuttered. 'You saw what happened here. They cleaned me out completely. Harry Larrimer let them take everything.'

'So it was Harry Larrimer,' the marshal mused. 'You do keep fancy company, Sid. I really hate to leave town and miss your hangin'.'

'Look, Marshal. . . !'

'I must be goin' now, Sid. Have a good journey.'

The gun-dealer came scrambling round the counter to grab the departing lawman by the arm.

'You can't leave me with him!' he cried. 'He'll kill me!'

The marshal pulled off the clawing hand. 'Rico only wants what's due to him. Then he'll be on his way, like a wise man. You got some money tucked away in a nice safe place, ain't you, Sid?'

'He's got a strongbox under the floor,' Rico said grimly, 'and I aim to get my share of what's in there. I've earned it.'

Will Tovey grinned. 'I'll bet you have, Rico. Did you recruit those braves who helped Larrimer's gang to disguise themselves and terrorize folk?'

The man nodded proudly.

'And was it you or Larrimer who gave them a few Winchesters?' the marshal asked.

'I did,' Rico answered happily.

'Then I reckon you're owed plenty,' the marshal told him as he left the building.

There was only the distance of a few feet between Sid Welland and his hired help. The gun-dealer backed off, edging along the counter to where a couple of old Colt Navy models were lying on display. Rico pointed the shotgun at his boss's chest.

'I ain't lookin' to shoot you, but I wants my money,' he said tersely. 'Now, let's go to the back room and lift up that floorboard. You pays me and I leaves.'

The gun-dealer looked longingly at the weapons that he had loaded only half an hour ago.

He licked his lips and did what Rico ordered. He walked slowly to the back room where he lived amid a welter of old furniture and an assortment of books that travelling salesmen had brought into town. Covered by the unwavering shotgun, he bent at the side of the pot-bellied stove and lifted the small plank that hid his store of money. With his back to Rico, he felt in his pocket for the bunch of keys and opened the box without having to take it from the gap under the floor.

There was a collection of five- and ten-dollar bills, some gold and silver coins, and a large gold watch that he had inherited from his father. He reached into the open box but removed none of those items. He picked up a double-barrelled derringer instead and turned on Rico.

The two weapons exploded almost at the same time. Sid Welland reeled back against the stove, shaking loose the chimney as he fell among a cloud of soot that turned the spraying blood into a muddy mess staining the floor and wall. The derringer dropped from his lifeless hand as Rico stood over him. The shotgun smoked slightly as the big man kicked the body aside and plunged his hand into the strongbox. He dragged everything out, looked around for a bag of some sort, and finally removed an old cushion from a chair to empty the stuffing on to the floor before using the cover to pack his loot.

He bled from a slight wound in the left arm,

but it was not important and he headed for the back door of the store where he could reach the corral in a few short yards to get his horse saddled and away.

His saddle was already on the porch, where he had left it ready for immediate use after the first trouble with the townsfolk. He had nothing else worth going back to his room for, and he picked up the heavy equipment to carry down to the corral.

As he turned, shotgun and bag in one hand, and saddle in the other, he found himself confronted by Marshal Tovey.

'Heard the noise,' the lawman said quietly, 'and reckoned you'd be leavin' by the back door. Just drop everything, Rico, and we can take our evenin' meal over at the jailhouse.'

The man stopped in his tracks. 'He tried to kill me, Marshal,' he explained. 'I just wanted my wages but he drew on me.'

'I heard the two shots, but we'll let the judge decide. Just drop everything and come along quiet-like.'

Rico slowly let the saddle fall to the ground. There was nobody else in sight. Just him and the lawman. He bent as if to lay the shotgun gently down, but suddenly straightened up, flung the bag of money at the marshal, and levelled the weapon.

Will Tovey staggered back, the heavy container

hitting him in the face as the gold and silver coins caught his nose and mouth. He threw up his hands blindly for a moment, fighting free of the bag and its contents. Rico had already cocked the shotgun and was pointing it at his chest. The lawman had no chance. There was no way that he could reach his holster before his opponent pulled the trigger. He braced himself for the hail of buckshot that would tear him apart.

A shot rang out. Not the blast of a scatter-gun but the clean, sharp noise of another Colt. Rico swore and turned in the direction of the sound as chips flew off the wall at his side. The mayor had come round the corner, a gun in his chubby hand and his face red with the exertion of running.

He fired again without aiming. Both shots had missed their target but it was time enough to save the marshal. He drew his own gun and shot Rico in the chest. The big man let out a roar of pain and rage as he dropped the shotgun but tried to reach for his Colt.

Will Tovey pulled the trigger again, and after a very slight pause, the man fell against the wooden wall of the store before sliding gradually to the ground. He lay moaning for a few moments as the mayor and the marshal stood over him. Then he died.

'That was a good move, Bob,' Will Tovey told the mayor thankfully as he picked up the bag of money. 'He had me for a sittin' gopher.'

'I'm sorry I missed,' the mayor panted, 'but I ain't fired a gun in years. What about Sid Welland?'

'I reckon that Rico did for him. We'll just have to go in and see.'

They came out of the store in a hurry. Sid Welland was certainly dead. As the two men walked towards the jailhouse, a small crowd began gathering to watch the doctor and the mortician hurrying to the scene of the action.

The marshal turned in the doorway of his office as he heard another noise in the distance. There was a large cloud of dust beyond the end of the main street. It was coming from the west with the clattering of hoofs as the long procession of townsmen rode into view, the mounts weary and the wagon of loot from the Indian reservation bringing up the rear. The butchers of Milo Creek had returned to Newton Crossing.

Twelve

The main street of Newton Crossing was crowded with people. The tired men still sat their horses, surrounded by the women who had encouraged them to go off only a few days before.

The same women were now telling them of the raiders who had looted the town, terrorized the citizens, and forced most of the stores to close through lack of goods and money to replenish stock. The bank was still shut, horses and saddlery were missing. The heroes of Milo Creek had returned to a place that was near despair.

Marshal Tovey stood at the side of the mayor and a few of the councilmen in the middle of the street. The blacksmith sat on his large horse, looking uneasy as he listened to how the raiders had posed as Indians to empty the town of defenders when they launched their attack. He was sweating heavily and rivulets ran down his dusty face like little rivers on the reddish skin.

'You done killed a lot of innocent folk,' the mayor said bleakly. He was still holding the pistol in his right hand and waving it dangerously at the mounted men. 'Them Indians never left the reservation. You got the law to answer to for this, Ned Floyd.'

The blacksmith tried to bluster. 'Them Indians is better out of the way!' he shouted. 'They're a menace to decent folk. And don't go blamin' me, Mr Mayor. I didn't start all this. It was Sid Welland sellin' them Winchesters.'

'Ah, yes,' the marshal said. 'The Winchesters. How many did you find at Milo Creek?'

'Well. . . .' The blacksmith looked around the group of horsemen for support. 'We didn't look for guns . . . .'

'You brought back animal pelts, blankets, a few sides of buffalo meat, and you didn't even look for valuable rifles?' the marshal sneered. 'You sure as hell is odd folk, Ned Floyd. It was the guns that sent you there in the first place. Now, get down off that horse and join me in the jailhouse.'

'You can't arrest me!' the blacksmith yelled. 'We're not havin' that, are we, fellas?'

He appealed to the men around him but there was a distinct lack of support. They sat glumly on their horses, silent as events moved against them. They had expected to be welcomed as heroes, but even their wives were now looking at them with a certain doubt.

'You won't be the only one in a jailhouse when the army arrive,' the mayor told them grimly. 'This is a government matter. Them Indians are under Washington's protection, and you done got yourselves in real hangin' trouble.'

'They can't hang us for killin' Indians,' someone murmured hopefully.

Will Tovey grinned. 'Would you like to take a wager on that? Now, I'm jailin' Ned Floyd. He was the leader of all this hootin' and a-hollerin'. If any of you has any objections to that, just make them now. As you can see, the mayor and me has already been doin' a bit of fancy shootin'. Welland and Rico are dead and the mortician's got a few caskets to spare for any more gun-happy folk.'

Ned Floyd slowly dismounted. He handed the reins of his horse to one of the other men and came to stand in front of the marshal.

'What will the army do?' he asked in a quiet voice.

'Hold an inquiry,' said the mayor. 'Then they'll make recommendations for tryin' folk before the courts. There could be a lotta hangings in this.'

'But we believed we were actin' right. There's a whole town involved.' Ned Floyd flung his arms wide to include everybody.

'Washington won't see it that way,' the mayor said. 'Now, tell me, Ned. What happened to the preacher at Milo Creek?'

'I didn't see no preacher,' the blacksmith said sullenly.

'Well, he was there,' the marshal told him. 'And you must have passed old Jesse Parker's place. Didn't he tell you that he was checkin' on the Indians for me?'

The blacksmith swallowed noisily. 'We didn't stop,' he said. Will Tovey looked at the other men but all of them were trying not to meet his eye.

'Well, get along to the jailhouse, Ned,' he said, 'and the rest of you can go home. The army will be questionin' everybody involved in the business, so don't try leavin' town. The stuff on that wagon can be put in the livery stable for now. It's stolen property.'

There was a stir of resentment but the lawman looked hard at the cowed group of men.

'If any of you want to argue the point, do it now,' he snapped.

Nobody answered, and as the marshal watched them, they gradually went to their various homes, leaving the main street almost deserted.

Only Ned Floyd remained. He stood on the porch of the jailhouse, his face a mixture of fear and anger. The marshal motioned him inside but the man stood his ground, blocking the doorway and with his hand near the butt of the old Colt at his side.

'If you draw that,' the marshal said quietly, 'I'll kill you.'

'You got me over a barrel, Will,' the man admitted. 'I'm not a fella to face down to anyone, and I don't aim to take the blame for somethin' I was only part of. You ain't puttin' me in jail without a fight. I owes that to myself. Sure, you'll draw faster than me, but I'd rather die here and now than go through all the fuss of bein' tried by some damned lawyers who didn't know what we went through in this town. We was believin' our families was threatened by Indians on the loose.'

'Ned,' the mayor said persuasively, 'them fellas would never have set off for Milo Creek if you hadn't been agitatin' like some angry horse tick. You led 'em on, fella; looted Welland's store and went gallopin' outa town on some highfalutin crusade. You got a lot to answer for, Ned. Just go inside quiet-like. The marshal don't want to shoot nobody. There's been enough killing.'

The blacksmith shook his head as if warding off a cloud of flies. 'Suppose them attacks had been Indian raids,' he countered. 'What would you have done then? We'd have come back to this town to a very different welcome. You wouldn't have been talkin' about the army and a trial. You'd have been makin' like we was heroes.'

'Well, you ain't heroes,' the marshal snapped, 'and I'm losin' patience. So get yourself inside before we have to lug your great fool carcass to the buryin' ground.'

A few people had come back on the street but

Ned Floyd's wife was not among them. The blacksmith looked for some support but met only hostility in the glances of folk who had been following him with enthusiasm a day or two past. He gave a low moan that could have been rage or despair, and drew his gun.

There was only one shot. Before he had even cocked the weapon, Marshal Tovey drew and fired with lightning speed. The bullet caught the blacksmith in the centre of the chest and he staggered forward as if trying to grapple with his killer. His foot slipped on the first step and he pitched head downward on to the dusty street.

The funeral took place the next day. The long procession of townsfolk walked behind the hearse towards the burial ground just outside town. It was a neat place with a host of white wooden crosses over grass-grown mounds. At one end was a memorial to the men who had died in the late war. A single black field-gun and a little pyramid of cannon-balls lay in front of it in dark contrast to the white stone plaque listing the names of those who served in the local Montana Volunteer Regiment.

There was no preacher to read the service but Doctor Earle stood in for him, a sturdy, moustachioed figure who read the funeral words in a clear bass voice to a congregation that seemed distracted by the whole business.

The marshal got some odd looks. Folk were not sure how to treat him. Sid Welland and Rico had already been buried, much to the professional joy of the mortician who was also looking forward to a series of trials that might result in a few hangings. His only worry was that it might all take place in another town.

People walked slowly away from the burial ground, talking in low voices and casting sideways glances at the mayor, the lawman, and the various members of the council. A pall of gloom lay over the stricken town.

The doctor hurried after the mayor to grab him roughly by the arm as he and the marshal reached the jailhouse, where they intended to have a quiet drink while they discussed events.

'Mayor, I have something urgent to say,' the doctor gasped as he halted the pair. 'I feel I have a duty to them folk at the reservation. I'm goin' out there to see if anyone has been left alive and is in need of help.'

The mayor halted in mid-stride. 'That's mighty handsome of you, Sam,' he said warmly. 'The marshal and me have talked about that, but we didn't like to ask you. I'd be greatly obliged if you'd do that thing. Will you take anybody with you?'

'My wife's a good nurse, and two of the other ladies have volunteered. I've plenty of supplies and we can make the journey in a couple of small wagons. I'd like to take back all those goods that were stolen. They'll certainly need the blankets.'

'I'll see to that,' Marshal Tovey said. 'And thanks for your offer, Doc.'

The three shook hands and Doctor Earle hurried off to harness up the animals and load the two light wagons with his supplies. He passed Myron Davis who was hurrying towards the jailhouse with a piece of paper fluttering in his hand. He gave it gleefully to the marshal.

'Straight from the fort!' he crowed triumphantly. 'There's a troop of cavalry on their way to Milo Creek. Then they'll come on here to hold all the men who went to the reservation so that Captain Duggan can question them.'

The lawman took the paper. 'Well, thank you for shoutin' the news to the entire town, Myron,' he said. 'You've saved me the job of tryin' to read your handwritin'. Any news from Platte Bridge?'

'No, I reckon they ain't fixed the wire yet.'

The marshal nodded his dismissal and the telegraph operator hurried back towards his office. The man suddenly stopped in his tracks and turned around.

'Oh, I forget to mention it, Marshal,' he said in his loud voice, 'The Reverend Thomas is ridin' into town. I caught sight of him comin' over the hill. Looks real tuckered-out, he does.'

Thirteen

The mayor and Will Tovey moved out to the centre of the main street where they could see the southern trail leading into Newton Crossing. There was a horseman in the distance, moving slowly as he slumped in the saddle. They hurried to meet him and were able to help the preacher down from the animal as he reached the first of the buildings. He took their aid gratefully, but did not forget to loosen the girth on the tired horse.

'I need something to eat and drink,' he said urgently. 'I'm so tired, I hardly know how I'm standing. Some hot coffee and a hunk of bread would seem like paradise right now.'

'Well, my wife has a good stew on the stove,' the mayor assured him, 'and I reckon there's enough of it for all of us. You'll join us, Will?'

'I won't say no.' The marshal grinned.

They sat in the parlour after the meal, the mayor

116

smoking a cigar while Will Tovey drank coffee
from a small china cup. The Reverend Thomas
was still eating from a plate of hot biscuits. It was
the lawman who summed up the position.

'So they're in the foothills,' he mused. 'The
army won't be here for a few days and the raiders
could have moved on by then. If we aim to have
our goods back, we've got to do somethin' now.
Not wait for the soldier-boys.'

'You could take all the townsmen with you,
Will,' the mayor said as he smoked. 'You'd sure
outnumber them.'

'True enough, and I reckon that the fellas in
this town need to do a little honest fightin' for a
change. Tell me, Ely, can we get through them
trees and surround the place?'

'Certain sure. You travel about a mile through
dense forest, but there is a trail. It's broad
enough for a wagon. Then you come to a clearing
with the hut about fifty yards away at the other
side of some sloping ground. The horses are
penned behind the cabin and the only way out is
either to climb up the slope to the rear or come
back along the trail. Once we hold the trail,
they're stuck there. You can't get horses through
the scrub. It's too dense.'

'Can they climb up towards the hills back of
the cabin?'

'Not that I can see. Those rocks are bare and
they just go way up to the snowline. If you block

117

the trail, spread your men out along the edge of the trees, you've got a clear field of fire.'

Will Tovey nodded. 'Trouble is,' he said, 'so have they. We could be there a coon's age if they've got supplies enough.'

'And if you attack,' the mayor said, 'you'll be crossin' open ground.'

They sat in silence for a while. All the biscuits were gone and the preacher was picking up the crumbs with his wetted fingertips.

'We could use the cannon,' he said suddenly.

The other two looked at him.

'What cannon?' the mayor asked in a puzzled tone.

'The one in the burial ground. All we need is powder and shot.'

Will Tovey looked at the reverend gentleman in surprise.

'Well, I for one don't know anythin' about guns,' he admitted, 'so we'd have to find somebody who did.'

The mayor nodded. He had been in the late war but had wisely served in the quartermaster's department.

'There's old Wally Finlay,' said the preacher. 'He was with the Montana Volunteers as a gunner.'

Marshal Tovey grinned. 'That may be so, Ely, but Wally never draws a sober breath.'

'Well, all the other townsfolk I know of were

118

infantry or cavalry. Wally should be able to load and fire the gun if we can haul it through those woods and place it fifty yards from the cabin. Even he couldn't miss at that range.'

The mayor chuckled. 'For a preacherman, you sure are one hell of a fire-eatin' son of a bitch, Ely Thomas.'

'Well, I was in the war, albeit as a preacher.'

The four men stood in the burial ground, peering at the old black cannon on its spoked wheels. It was quite free from dirt, as was the monument to the fallen that stood behind it. The barrel was of iron, pitted on the surface but still looking good.

Wally Finlay's pale-blue eyes were alert as he ran a gnarled and slightly shaky hand over the metalwork.

'It sure is a fine piece of castin',' he said admiringly. 'I reckon that General Washington felt right proud of it.'

'You mean that this thing is just a relic from the Foundin' Fathers?' Will Tovey asked in disgust.

'What the hell do you think?' Wally grinned. 'It ain't bin fired since then, or maybe in that other war against the English. The one where they burned down the White House and old Andy Jackson got hisself famous. This is old cast iron and like to blow apart if you put too much of a charge in it.'

119

He went over to the little pyramid of black-painted cannon-balls and kicked them contemptuously with his worn boot.

'And they ain't no use either. Just for display like the gun. They're bigger than the bore of this piece. When the army gave the town these, they weren't givin' nothin' valuable away. The army don't do things like that, Marshal.'

The little preacher shook his head sadly. 'Well, there goes an idea. I suppose we'll have to think again.'

The town drunk licked his lips and looked at the other three men. It was not often that the town worthies were at his mercy.

'Well,' he said with apparent reluctance, 'I ain't sayin' as how it couldn't be made to fire. It just needs a bit of thinkin' about. I'd have to check it over for safety and we'd need coarse powder, and some shot. A thirsty job under a sun like this.'

They took the hint and led the man to the nearest saloon where after three beers and three whiskies, Wally was feeling more optimistic. He explained all the technicalities and also suggested that the local stonemason could make shot from roughly shaped stones. After several more drinks, the other were equally enthusiastic.

Just as the sun was setting behind the snow-covered hills to the west, the gun was ready for testing. Two draught horses had been harnessed to the piece and it was dragged from the burial ground to an open space outside town where it pointed to an empty landscape of tangled grass and stunted trees.

Two stone cannon-balls had already been prepared, most of the town stood at a safe distance, and old Wally Finlay was fussing around, important for the first time in years. He had probed the barrel, cleared the touch-hole, and greased the wheels and the elevating-screw.

As everybody stood anxiously, he placed a bag of powder in the muzzle and pushed it down with a hastily made ramrod. Then he rolled down the ball, wrapped in a piece of sacking so that it fitted snugly. He came round to the rear of the gun and took a long goose-quill. As they all watched, he plunged it into the touch-hole until it pierced the bag of powder. He took some more powder, filled the touch-hole, and looked around for approval.

'Ready for shootin', Marshal,' he said proudly. 'But remember now, I ain't guaranteein' nothin'. This here powder is too fine. It's for pistols and suchlike.'

'It's all that was left in Welland's store,' Will Tovey snapped impatiently. 'Just get on with it.'

The old drunk picked up the long stick to which he had attached the slow match. He blew heavily until the dull glow brightened, and looked round at the admiring crowd.

'Better hold them horses!' he warned.

121

A couple of men grabbed the reins of the draught animals who were grazing peacefully in the background. Some of the women covered their ears while the children jumped up and down with excitement.

Wally gave another blow on the slow match, and holding the pole as far away as possible, he applied it to the touch-hole.

There was a bright flash just a moment before a satisfying roar as the field-piece jumped backwards and a blast of flame and heat shot from the barrel. Will Tovey stared into the distance, and sure enough, a spurt of dirt leapt up from the ground about a hundred or more yards away. A cheer went up and everyone grinned happily at the success.

While the children rushed to pick up fragments of the stone ball, Will Tovey patted Wally on the back. He was pleased with the outcome but something was nagging away at the back of his mind. He looked round the crowd, but one face was missing. The marshal quietly detached himself from the people who were gathered round his colleagues. He walked back into town and found what he expected to find. One man was saddling a horse, ready to depart from Newton Crossing.

'I don't want you leavin' town, Myron,' the lawman said quietly as he rounded the corner by the corral in which the telegraph operator kept his horse.

'Oh, I was just off to look at the line towards Platte Bridge, Marshal,' the man stammered hurriedly. He was wearing a gun but made no effort to reach for it.

'Well, I'd rather you spent the next few days safely in the jailhouse. That way, maybe we can take them raiders by surprise.'

The man blanched. 'Marshal,' he said fearfully, 'you don't reckon as how I had anythin' to do with what's been happenin' round here? That just ain't possible.'

'I ain't sayin ' you did and I ain't sayin' you didn't. But I'm takin' precautions, fella, and you're stayin' in town until we get back.'

'But, Marshal. . . !'

'Come on, son. Let's go. You see, I got a nasty mind and you control the telegraph. I looked up some old Wanted bills and I sees that Harry Larrimer was a telegraphist in the Confederate army. I just can't take the chance of you warnin' them raiders. If I'm wrong, I'll apologize real handsome. But if I'm right, Myron, and you has been helpin' them raiders, then you're for a trial and a hangin'. That's a promise.'

Fourteen

It was a jubilant force that set off from Newton Crossing. They rode at a slow pace, escorting the field-gun that was dragged by the two heavy horses followed by a wagon that bore food, ammunition, and water. Will Tovey had picked his men carefully. He only took a little over twenty, knowing that the larger the number, the more difficult it would be to organize things, and the longer the journey would take.

He also felt ill at ease with the crowd that had been to Milo Creek. Some of them were with him now, and he hated his need of them.

The weather was warm and cloudy, with a hint of rain in the air. The little preacher led the way, important for the first time in his life and with a self-satisfaction that was only matched by the smug bearing of old Wally Finlay. The town drunk sat on the wagon, next to the driver, knowing that he was the one indispensable member of the expedition.

124

They camped for the night at the same place that Ely Thomas had used on his journey behind the raiders. The rain came down heavily, putting out their fires and leaving everyone miserable and sleepless. It cleared just before dawn and they were glad to be on their way again. Small birds followed their trail, picking at the myriad insects that the hoofs and wheels disturbed on the ground. The sun rose high in a sky that gradually became cloudless. As they warmed up, the men became more cheerful, and Wally fell off the wagon twice as he supplied himself with whiskey from some secret source that was shared with nobody else.

The line of tall pine trees eventually appeared in the distance, dark and forbidding with the sloping hills and high mountains beyond. The talking stopped as they realized that they were reaching a point when fighting would start and people could get killed. It would not be like Milo Creek where defenceless women and children would be shot down easily. It would be a fight against men to whom killing was a way of life. Will Tovey looked round at his suddenly silent followers and smiled ruefully. He had a strong feeling that if things got too rough, he could be on his own. Only the preacher seemed a tough enough character to stand up when real trouble began.

Ely Thomas pointed out the gap in the trees

where a trail snaked through towards the hills. The marshal called a halt and told the men how things were to be from that point onwards.

'We leave the horses and wagon here,' he said. 'Noise has got to be kept down if we're goin' to take 'em by surprise. You'll fix ropes to the gun and drag it along. Powder and shot will be carried by all of us, and that way we'll keep things as quiet as possible. We'll also block the trail with the wagon, so that if they do manage to get on their horses, they won't be able to edge past it easily. These trees are too close together to let animals through, so they'd have to stick to the path. If any of them do escape, they'll be on foot.'

'How far is this clearing?' somebody asked uneasily.

'About a mile,' the preacher answered. 'The trees are dense and they won't see us approach. The clearing is a small one and if we place the gun a little way back from the entrance of the trail, there'll be a good view of the cabin. Wally should be able to fire straight into it once he has the range.'

Will Tovey nodded. 'The rest of us will spread out along the edge of the trees and open fire at the same time,' he said. 'Not as easy as shootin' Indians while they're still half-asleep, but you shouldn't have too much trouble.'

He had chosen the right tone. None of the men was eager to argue with him. Wally Finlay supervised the hitching of the ropes to the field-gun and the long drag began through the overgrown trail between tall, dark trees that seemed empty of animal and bird life. Their progress was slow, and even the marshal and the preacher had each to carry a cannon-ball. Wally was the only person with a light load. He walked jauntily with the ramrod and linstock on his shoulder and a broad smile on his face.

They stopped about a hundred yards from the clearing, resting while Will Tovey and the preacher went ahead to see what was happening in the open space beyond the trail.

It was late afternoon by now and smoke was coming from the stone chimney at the end of the large cabin which was constructed of heavy logs, expertly joined and covered with lines of moss that had gathered over the years. There were three men chopping wood in front of the building while a fourth was washing himself with the aid of a wooden pail and large bar of yellow soap. The door of the cabin was open and voices could be heard across the clearing.

'Well, they certainly ain't expectin' visitors,' the marshal whispered, 'but we'll have to bring that gun up quietly.'

'We could wait until nightfall,' the preacher suggested.

'Too risky to work in the dark. No, I think we should go ahead now, while we still have daylight. One shot should be enough to finish 'em. If they try makin' for them slopes, we can pick them off with rifles, and if they take to their horses, it'll be even worse for them. I reckon we're gonna get all our goods and money back without no trouble.'

'I pray you're right, Marshal.'

The two men went silently back, joined the others and explained the position. Some of the powder and shot was left on the trail while Wally loaded the gun ready for use. It was then dragged the rest of the way, as quietly as possible, but not silently enough to avoid being heard by one of the raiders. He stopped chopping wood, listened for a while, and then gestured his companions to be still. They stood motionless for a moment, saw or heard some movement on the trail, and ran for the cabin in a panic.

Some of the marshal's men fanned out along the edge of the tree line and opened fire at the cabin. The door slammed shut while shots were returned through shuttered windows. A barrage from both sides sent smoke and bullets across the open space while Wally sighted the gun.

'Ready, Marshal,' he said as he blew on the linstock.

'What are you aimin' for?' Will Tovey asked.

'I ain't fussy with a piece like this,' the old man replied. 'Just so I hit the cabin fair and square.'

Will Tovey stepped back into the trees as the

gunner touched the glowing match to the priming powder. The gun jumped viciously on its wheels as a belch of flame and smoke flew from the muzzle.

They all let out a moan as a long furrow was torn into the earth several feet in front of the cabin. No damage had been done but the firing from the building came to a halt.

'That was one hell of a shot!' the marshal shouted angrily.

'I told you the powder was all wrong,' Wally snapped back. 'And I can't overload it in case the barrel bursts. This ain't a safe piece to use. It should be back where we found it.'

'Well, try again.'

'I aim to, but they'll have to drag it back in line. And have 'em pull it back down the trail a few yards so I don't get shot in the ass while I'm loadin' the blame thing.'

Willing hands dragged the gun along while Wally swabbed it out and loaded another small bag of powder. Ely Thomas tried to persuade him to use a larger charge, but he was pushed away angrily. The old man rammed down another stone ball, elevated the gun a little higher this time, and then waved everyone back. He touched the linstock to the pan and the gun roared once again.

The thing kicked as before, one wheel slipping on a rut and swinging the piece askew on the trail. They all leaned forward, regardless of the renewed shooting from the cabin. The ball hit the corner of the building, just below the roof. Large chunks of timber flew off and part of the roof support vanished in a cloud of dust.

A ragged cheer went up and the firing stopped for several moments. Both sides seemed stunned by the success. Wally motioned for the gun to be brought back to its position again. His face was glowing with pride at mastering the ancient weapon. He reloaded and aimed carefully along the barrel. His alcoholic breath came heavily as he sighted for range and elevation.

'Stand back!' he shouted, and touched off the charge.

The cannon roared again and they all waited in vain for the fall of shot.

'Where the hell did that go?' Will Tovey asked.

'I think it went over the roof and landed among the rocks,' the preacher ventured. 'I saw some dirt being kicked up on the slope. You set it too high, Wally.'

'That was a rangin' shot,' the old man said grandly. 'One in front, one behind, and the last one square on. That's the proper way of doin' things.'

Will Tovey was almost going to point out that the second shot was better than the third, but pulled himself up in time. There was no point in antagonizing their gunner.

'Well done, Wally,' he said calmly.

The gun was loaded and trained a few minutes later. Both sides were still firing wildly at each other but some of the attackers eased off to see what their cannon would do at this attempt.

It went off with the same satisfying noise as before, a mass of choking smoke enshrouding the onlookers for a few moments. When it cleared, they let out a cheer. The ball had gone straight through into the cabin after splitting two of the logs and pulling them away from the corner joints.

There was a long silence before the door of the structure opened cautiously and a stick topped by a dirty piece of cloth was waved by a nervous hand.

'We're comin' out!' a voice called. 'Just hold your fire!'

'Throw your guns out first!' the marshal shouted back. 'Any tricks and you'll get another shot!'

Wally was already reloading the gun, proud of his work and grinning broadly.

Several Winchesters clattered to the ground in front of the cabin. A few revolvers followed along with three shotguns. Will Tovey stepped forward into the clearing to tell the surrendering men what to do next. Before he could speak, they began to troop out of the cabin with their hands in the air. They were a very docile bunch of raiders now. Completely demoralized by the cannon and covered with dust and smoke, they looked a pretty sheepish lot.

There were ten of them, gathering in a group in front of the open door. Will Tovey drew his gun, and as he did so, a wild fusillade of shots rang out. He stood frozen for a moment before realizing that it was his own men who were firing.

He waved frantically to stop them, but it was too late. The prisoners were mown down where they stood. Some tried to run back to the cabin but died as they crossed the threshold. It was all over in a moment. Ten dead or dying men on the ground amid their surrendered weapons. It was a whooping, triumphant bunch of townsmen who emerged from cover with smoking guns to run among the corpses and search them. They were like a flock of hungry vultures.

Ely Thomas and the marshal looked at each other. There was nothing that either of them could do. Wally joined them, wiping his face with a dirty cloth.

'That sure as hell was a piece of shootin, folks,' he said with satisfaction.

'The cannon or the massacre?' the preacher asked dryly.

'Both. There won't be no time wasted on a trial and a hangin' now. All finished, neat as neat. Mind you, folks like a good hangin'. Shame there ain't just one of them we could have gotten back to town alive.'

The marshal had been inspecting the bodies.

'You might get your hangin' yet, Wally,' he said. 'There are two missin'. Harry Larrimer and the tall fella we saw back in the jailhouse.'

Fifteen

Will Tovey wasted no time. He ran to the rear of the cabin and drew out one of the restless horses. There was no time to saddle it, and after getting control of the rope halter, he leapt on its back and headed down the trail, skirting the cannon as he did so.

The animal was difficult, not used to being guided without a bit and with a strange rider using spurs relentlessly. The ground was rough and the marshal was desperate to head off the two men who would be running through the trees to come out where they could steal a couple of mounts from those that had been left with the wagon at the edge of the forest.

He hoped that he was ahead of them, but if they had sneaked out of the cabin before their companions had surrendered, they might be well on their way to safety.

His only hope was that they had let the others

leave by the door while they climbed through a
rear window and crawled along the stony slope of
low bushes amid patches of moss. They would
skirt round until reaching the line of trees and
then head out to the open range, probably guessing that horses would be hitched somewhere
close to the beginning of the trail.

The lawman had not ridden an unsaddled
horse since he was a boy on the family farm in
Wyoming. He was glad when the trail ended as
the trees petered out and the wide range lay
ahead in a long valley of patchy grass that sloped
off towards the east.

The horses were still there, hitched to long
ropes stretched between trees and grazing
contentedly while they waited. He dismounted,
tied the animal to one of the ropes, and ran along
to tighten the girth of his own mount. There was
no sign of any movement from the trees as he
backed his horse under the shelter of a large pine
that was surrounded by tall ferns. He checked his
shotgun, rifle, and pistol as he waited patiently
for the men he was hunting.

His lack of movement brought the disturbed
birds back to their quarrelling among the upper
branches of the trees. A few jackrabbits came
closer, cropping the grass around the tethered
horses while flies hovered around.

Everything looked undisturbed and the
marshal easily detected a sudden noise in the

undergrowth. He quietly unholstered his rifle and cocked it.

Somebody was coming through the trees, furtively but rustling the scrub as he moved. The lawman put a gentle hand over the nose of his mount and listened intently for the direction of the sounds.

A figure emerged from the forest, tall and young, with a long, anxious face marred by a heavy unshaven jaw. It was the man who had been in the jailhouse. His clothes were streaked with dirt from the bombardment of the cabin as he stood at the edge of the wood, looking carefully around before approaching the line of tethered animals.

Will Tovey hesitated. He could easily shoot the man from this distance, but it was really the leader he wanted. Harry Larrimer was the mastermind, and he was the one who had to be caught. The marshal listened for some other movement among the trees, but could hear nothing.

The shot took him by surprise. The tall man was just reaching out to unhitch a horse when he staggered to his knees, dropping the saddle-bag he was carrying. He tried to recover but slipped down again, feeling for the Colt at his waist but without enough strength to draw it. Will Tovey watched quietly from the cover of the trees.

There was a long pause, only broken by the

movement of the restless horses. They were tugging at their ropes, startled by the shot after so long a rest in the quietness of the range.

The marshal waited as another man came out of the trees. He moved silently, an experienced woodsman, and he too carried a full saddle-bag. A Winchester was in his right hand and he looked carefully around before bending to pick up the saddle-bag that the fallen man had been carrying. He slung it over his shoulder and began to unhitch a horse for his own use.

It was now that the marshal made his move. He spurred his mount out of the trees and pointed the Winchester at the startled man.

'Drop the gun, Larrimer!' he shouted. 'You're goin' back to Newton Crossing.'

Harry Larrimer turned slowly. His right hand still held the rifle, but with one saddle-bag on his shoulder and the other in his left hand, he was at a total disadvantage.

His face was a study in anger for a moment, but then he grinned, the white teeth showing brightly against the dark moustache.

'Well, I reckon as how you must be the lawman of that little town we just visited,' he said cheerfully. 'We never did get to meet back there. And you sure have me hog-tied. Suppose we do ourselves a deal, Marshal?'

'What deal?'

'I got two saddle-bags here. Both full of money

and fit to bustin' at the seams. One for you and one for me. How about it?'

'All I gotta do is shoot you and I get both of them,' Will Tovey said quietly.

'Ah, but you won't,' the raider answered. 'I checked your town before makin' a social call. They all agree that you was one honest lawman. I reckon you want to take me in for trial and see that I get hanged all nice and legal. Right?'

'Right. A lotta folk died because of you.'

'Folks is dyin' all the time. I seen more dyin' in the war than you would believe. So I ain't interested in nobody but me from now on. And I ain't aimin' to go a-hangin', Marshal. Not nohow.'

'Just drop the gun. I won't ask again.'

The man shrugged and let the Winchester fall to the ground.

'You're missin' out on a good deal, Marshal,' he said. 'All you gotta do is to shove this saddle-bag on your horse and let me ride out. Poor Fred ain't talkin' and I'll be long gone to Wyomin' and points south. You'll have a nice little somethin' for your old age. How about it?'

Will Tovey shook his head. He was watching the man carefully and wishing that some of the others would arrive to back him.

'No deal,' he said tersely. 'Just drop the bags, and do it slow.'

Harry Larrimer grimaced. He let the saddle-bags fall to the ground, glancing at them regretfully as they lay in an untidy heap at his feet. He was just about to speak again when a solitary figure appeared at the mouth of the trail. It was Preacher Thomas, angry and flushed at the conduct of the men back in the clearing. He stopped short when he recognized the raid leader, and a thankful smile lit up his face.

'Well, at least one thing decent's come of it,' he said as he approached the two men. He noticed the other body and bent over it to check for life while murmuring a prayer.

'That was Fred,' the marshal explained. 'Larrimer didn't want to share the loot with him.'

The preacher looked at the killer. 'I don't normally like to think of hangings,' he said, 'but you certainly try the patience of any Christian man.'

He moved behind the prisoner and took the pistol from the man's belt. Larrimer also had a knife tucked into the pocket of his trail coat and the preacher removed that while he was at it.

Others were beginning to arrive now, burdened down with the goods they had recovered from the cabin. They were cheerful, all feeling like heroes as they confronted the leader of the gang that had raided their town.

Marshal Tovey found himself pushed aside as they gathered round Harry Larrimer. Blows were struck and the man was kicked to the ground. The lawman, assisted by the little preacher, tried to stop them, but the anger of the townsmen was too much. Will Tovey found himself pushed against the trees while little Mr Thomas slipped on the grass and was trampled underfoot as the mob of shouting men dragged Harry Larrimer towards one of the pines that had a low, strong branch.

A rope was thrown over it, and before Will Tovey could even break free and make himself heard, the raider was hoisted up and left kicking as he spun round on the end of the halter. A loud animal cry split the air as the triumphant townsmen stood around and watched their prisoner die. The marshal cursed and the little preacher wept.

Sixteen

Newton Crossing was rejoicing. The heroes had returned with all the stolen goods. The saloons did a record business as celebrations went on into the night amid noise and confusion as the crowds moved about the main street and guns were fired into the air, frightening the horses and annoying the few people who were trying to sleep.

Marshal Tovey sat in the jailhouse, ignoring it all. He had watched the loading of the wagons with the recovered goods. He had supervised the return of the cannon to the burial ground, and he had made sure that Wally Finlay got enough money to drink himself into oblivion. He had let them all shake his unresisting hand and slap him on the back. But his eyes were full of contempt as he retired from the scene after noting the collection of telegraph equipment that had been found in the cabin.

He was drinking coffee now, sitting behind his

desk in the light of a single oil-lamp. Myron
Davis lay on the bunk in the narrow cell, restlessly scraping his feet against the floor as he
whistled mournfully through bad teeth.

'Stop that noise!' the lawman shouted.

The man jumped up and came to the bars. 'You
should be lettin' me outa here, Marshal. I ain't
done nothin' wrong!' he shouted back. 'The telegraph company is goin' to be real mad when they
hears about this.'

'They'll be real mad when I tell them that you
was in touch with Larrimer's gang and he was
usin' the telegraph to keep in touch with you. You
passed on to him everything that was happenin'
here, and I aim to let the visitin' judge deal with
it. I reckon as how you're for a hangin', boy.'

'That's all lies! Them wires was cut. I couldn't
get in touch with the Fort or Platte Bridge.'

The marshal got out of his chair and crossed to
the cell. Myron Davis backed away in case things
got violent.

'The army will be here soon,' the lawman said
grimly. 'They can tell us a bit more, Myron, and
they're gonna be real upset about all them reservation Indians who died just so that this town
could be robbed. What was your cut goin' to be?'

The man shook his head violently. 'I wasn't
involved,' he said. 'I swear, Marshal, I wasn't in
on it. And you can't prove no different.'

Will Tovey knew that the man was correct.

Without evidence from one of the raiders, it was unlikely that any court would convict young Myron Davis. That was why he had needed to take Harry Larrimer alive. He went despondently back to his chair and sipped the coffee. Gunfire in the street outside left him completely indifferent. He no longer cared about the activities of the townsfolk.

The morning was colder as the wind came off the distant, snow-capped mountains. There were high clouds with a hint of sleety rain as the troop of cavalry entered Newton Crossing. A dust-covered lieutenant was in the lead; young and pale-faced as though new to service in wild country. A captain rode at his side, wearing infantry buttons and riding on a staff officer's saddle. He was an older man, dark and broad with pale-grey eyes under a hat that showered dust as he took it off to wipe his brow.

There was a woman riding near the rear of the troop, alongside a wagon that bore supplies. She was on a mule, wrapped against the chill and with an old bonnet pulled over her face.

The marshal and the mayor went out to greet them, waiting patiently for the officers to dismount before shaking hands and welcoming them to Newton Crossing. Billets were already arranged in the schoolhouse, and while somebody led the soldiers in that direction, Preacher

Thomas came forward and took the bridle of the woman's mule to lead her to his own home where his wife would care for her needs. She was obviously an Indian and nobody else was likely to make the effort.

The mayor led the two officers to his room over the store. He plied them with hot coffee and whiskey while the council gathered round to hear about events.

The captain explained his presence with the cavalry troop while the young lieutenant maintained a respectful silence.

'My name is Duggan, Mr Mayor,' the swarthy man said in a rich, deep voice. 'Colonel West has appointed me to investigate this massacre. Lieutenant Wilder here is in charge of cavalry operations. I need hardly tell you that this is a very serious affair. So, before we go any further, I would like to hear how it all started.'

Bob Harris quietly explained how the supposed Indian raids had built up and what lay behind it all. The marshal occasionally added a few words while the listening officers nodded silently at their recital.

'Well, I think you've made that all very clear, gentlemen,' he said when they had finished. 'Now I'll tell you what we met at Milo Creek. Most of the Indians are dead. Only a few have survived so far. Seven women, six children, and an old man. Your local doctor is out there now, looking after them, and doing as good a job as a man could do. Given the circumstances.

'My task now is to question all the local men who took part. I need your permission for that, Mr Mayor, and if I have enough evidence, then I will report back to the Commission for Indian Affairs and they will take the necessary legal action. The local Indian agent, a reverend gentleman, was shot to death. His home was looted as were the government stores that he had in his custody. That is a direct crime against the Washington government, but I doubt that we'll get anywhere.'

'Why not?' asked the mayor. 'We all know who did the killings.'

The captain shrugged. 'It's the legal position,' he said grimly. 'Knowing is one thing. Proving is another. I doubt if any of those involved are going to tell tales out of school. They'll stick together and leave us to prove it. And we can't unless somebody gives names.'

The banker slapped his hand on the desk top. 'That's all lawyer rubbish!' he shouted. 'We know who went out there, who did the killings, and who came back here with Indian goods. All lawyer talk!'

'I am a lawyer,' the captain snapped. 'That's why I'm here.' He turned to the marshal. 'What's your opinion of all this?' he asked.

Will Tovey got out of his chair and crossed to the window.

'The street's kinda empty,' he said quietly.
'Plenty of womenfolk and a few older men, but all
the able-bodied ones who raided the Indian reservation are missin'. I reckon they left town at
about the time you soldier-boys arrived. They
ain't stupid, Captain, and they'll stay away until
you leave.'

The officer nodded. 'I expected that. It always
happens and I always have to report back that
nobody knows anything. The trouble with this
particular case is that three white men were
killed. That will cause a stir back in Washington.
They'll want action.'

'Three white men!' the mayor exclaimed. 'We
know about Cavetty and Blackett, but who is the
other one?'

'An old settler by the name of Jesse Parker.
They killed him on their way to Milo Creek, and
burned down his cabin. His wife hid out back and
we brought her into town. She recognized the
man who shot Jesse. Your local blacksmith.'

'I had to shoot him,' the marshal said. 'He was
certainly the leader of all the trouble. Couldn't
wait to go kill himself a few Indians. I'm sure
sorry about Jesse, though. He was a good man,
and a friend.'

The meeting rambled on, all the council men
determined to have their say, but some of them
were relieved that the captain's investigations
might come to nothing. A town with half the men

in jail did not hold any appeal to the store-
owners.

When the conference broke up, Will Tovey
followed Captain Duggan into the open air. He
took him by the arm.

'What can you tell me about the telegraph line,
Captain?' he asked.

'It's working, as far as I know,' the man replied.

The lawman explained what part the line had
played in the problems of the town while the officer listened patiently.

'I see your point, Marshal,' he said, 'but back at
the fort, we never heard tell of the line being
down. No messages came in from Newton
Crossing or Platte Bridge and we had none to
send. The first call we got was the one that
brought us here. If this operator of yours was
working with the Larrimer gang, I don't see how
you're going to prove it.'

Will Tovey pulled a wry face. 'Could an experienced operator like Harry Larrimer tap into the
line without cuttin' the wires?' he asked.

'I don't see why not. And this Davis fellow kept
him informed? Is that how you think it was
done?'

'Yes, but I can't prove it.'

'Your job is like mine. We may know who's
guilty but we can't always find enough evidence
for judge and jury to do anything about it.' The
captain slapped the heavy gloves against his leg

in sudden anger. 'It annoys me beyond measure,' he said. 'I saw all those dead bodies back there, and you and I both know who killed them. But what the hell can we do? At least you were able to shoot one or two of them. I can't even have that pleasure.'

The marshal nodded glumly and went back to his office. His solitary prisoner looked up eagerly as the door opened.

'How long are you keepin' me here, Marshal?' he yelled.

Will Tovey crossed to the desk and took out the cell keys.

'I reckon you have the right of it, Myron,' he said sadly, 'and I'm lettin' you out so that you can go back to your office and keep sendin' messages up and down the line. But I'll tell you this, boy. I figure you for bein' as guilty as hell. You and Larrimer kept in touch, cut off this town, arranged that raid, and got all them Indians killed. I know it sure as I know that Wally Finlay is a drunk.'

He threw open the cell door. 'Now, get the hell outa my sight. You stink up the jailhouse. And remember this, Myron. If ever the folks in this town hear about what you did, they'll lynch you for certain sure. They already done it to Larrimer after killin' all his men. And you ain't a fightin' fella like they was. You'd go easy.'

The man was just about to step out of the cell

but the marshal's words made him recoil.

'You ain't tellin' the folks?' he asked fearfully.

Will Tovey grinned. 'They know you're in jail, but I ain't the gossipin' type. And like I said, I can't prove what you did. But the mayor knows, and the preacher. And they got wives. It's a small town, son, so what do you think of somebody talkin' while they're 'tendin' Bible class or doin' the marketin'?'

He grabbed the young man roughly by the arm, dragged him from the cell and propelled him to the door of the jailhouse. It was open, and a woman stood in the entrance as if just about to come in. She looked at the two men with a blank expression as the telegraph operator scuttled past her into the street. When he had gone, she entered and closed the door behind her.

The marshal immediately recognized her. It was Mary Parker, the Indian widow of old Jesse who had been killed by the blacksmith. He sat her down, poured out some coffee, and listened to her story about how their home had been attacked by the mob on its way to Milo Creek.

'I hid out back,' she said as she concluded her tale. 'Poor Jesse was beyond help. They had no call to do that, Marshal.'

'No, lass, they hadn't, and I killed Ned Floyd, if it's any consolation. How are you managin' now?'

'The Reverend Thomas and his wife have taken me in, and I can stay with them till my boy comes

home. I was thinking of going back to my own
people, but it's been too long. I've got no close kin
there now, Marshal. Besides, I don't feel like
ending my days on a reservation like a caged
animal.'

Will Tovey nodded. 'I wish I could help, Mary,'
he said, 'but I can't even punish those who caused
all this.'

'Like that young fella who just left?'

'Yes, and all those who went to Milo Creek. The
army will ask questions and the Indian Agency
will get a report, but you can't punish a whole
town. It just ain't possible.'

She nodded her understanding, the immobile
face giving no sign of any emotions that she
might be feeling. The marshal sat down and
drank his coffee after she had gone. He was feeling rather useless as he took out a deck of cards
and started playing patience.

It was about half an hour later that he heard
some odd sort of commotion on the main street.
He looked out of the window to see a small group
of women arguing with the mayor who stood on
the steps of his store. Angry words were being
exchanged and the lawman decided he had better
go out and see what was happening.

The women were complaining about the
absence of Doctor Earle. People in the town who
needed his services were being neglected while
he went out to look after Indians. Just as the

marshal was about to intervene, Captain Duggan appeared and the women quickly dispersed in case he started enquiring for the whereabouts of their husbands again. The marshal had judged it well. Hardly a member of the gang that had gone to Milo Creek was to be seen about the town.

He returned to his office with a sigh of relief.

Doctor Earle arrived back a couple of hours later. The afternoon shadows were long as a weak sun filtered through high clouds. The sleet had stopped, leaving a few tiny patches on roofs and a chill in the air.

The two small wagons pulled up outside the jailhouse. The doctor left the three ladies to take the rigs round to the stables while he entered the marshal's office. He looked tired and damp, needing a shave as well as a wash. He took the whiskey thankfully and drew a bentwood chair over to the stove.

'It was worse than anything I've seen since the war,' he said as he hugged the glass between cold hands. 'A complete slaughter of unarmed people. I've done the best I can, and I think the few that are left will pull through. I see the army's arrived in town, for all the good they can do.'

The marshal told him what had been happening and the doctor listened as he finished the drink and spread out his hands to the warmth of the stove.

'Life just ain't fair,' Will Tovey finished in an angry voice. 'There just ain't no justice.'

The doctor managed a slight grin. 'Oh, I don't know about that, Will,' he said with a certain relish. 'You see, them Indians could never have raided anybody, even if they'd wanted to. They was all as ill as could be. The Milo Creek reservation was riddled with smallpox.'

Seventeen

The marshal had lit the oil-lamp that hung from the ceiling. Its double burner gave a pleasant glow to the warm office.

'You mean that they was all ill when the shootin' started?' he asked.

'They sure as hell was. Lying there in their beds and nursed by the Reverend Blackett as best he could. They were a pretty sick lot of folk, and had been for a couple of weeks. It was not what we of the medical profession call malignant smallpox. The proper term for their ailment is the *discrete* condition. Most of them would have recovered in the normal way. A few of the children or the old people might have passed on, but Indians is a tough folk, and left alone, most would have pulled through.'

The marshal stirred uneasily. 'Smallpox is easily caught, ain't it?' he asked anxiously.

The doctor smiled. 'It certainly is, and all those

153

brave fellows who raided the Indians and took
away blankets as well as robbing the corpses of
everything they could, will soon know all about
it. I reckon as how there are going to be a lot of
very sick folk in town very shortly.'

'I think it's already started,' Will Tovey said.
'The women were wantin' to know where the hell
you was. I thought their menfolk had left town,
but now I reckon that they're more like to be lyin'
a-bed feelin' like they was due to meet their
Maker.'

'I do hope so, Will. I do hope so.'

'What about me though? I've been mixin' with
'em.'

'You went with me to Miles City two years
back. When the railroad was laid there.
Remember?'

'Sure, I recall the visit. And you got me drunk.'

'Exactly. Because that was the only way I could
get you to go along to their new fancy hospital
and be vaccinated. Just like I'd like to have everybody treated. You're safe from smallpox, my lad.
Safe as a man can be. You and me can stand by
and watch nature take its revenge. The soldier-
boys are safe too.' He chuckled.

'Did Captain Duggan know about this?' the
marshal asked.

'No, I was busy treating the injured while he
was there. It was only a while later that I spotted
the symptoms on some of the dead. Those poor

folks sure had a rough deal.'

The marshal saw the doctor to the door and stood watching as the medical man walked down the street towards his home. One or two women accosted him as he was turning the corner in the gathering darkness. Doctor Earle was going to be a busy man.

As he stood on the wooden porch, Will Tovey breathed deeply to get rid of the dizziness that the whiskey had caused. He looked up and down the street and noticed that a mule was tethered outside the telegraph office. It was waiting patiently, laden with baggage that left hardly enough room for a rider to get a grip in the saddle. He recognized the animal and waited to see what would happen next.

The telegraph office was lighted, with the door closed against the coldness of the evening. It opened after a few minutes and a woman came out. She untethered the mule, climbed laboriously into the saddle and turned the animal to come up the street to the northern end of the town.

She was easy to recognize in the light of the jailhouse as she drew level with the open doorway.

'Evenin', Mary,' the marshal greeted her. 'Leavin' town so soon?'

She stopped the mule and her calm Indian face broke into a very slight smile.

155

'Towns are not for me, Marshal,' she said slowly. 'I've done all I want to do here.'

'I wish you well, then, and if there's anythin' I can ever do to help, just call on me.'

'You did help, Marshal,' she said softly, 'when you released that red-haired man from the jailhouse.'

She kicked the mule in its flank and the animal walked slowly on. The marshal returned to his office, closed the door, and sat down at the desk. He was suddenly feeling a lot better.

He had noticed the blood on her hand and the locks of stained red hair that were fastened to her belt.